A Feather of
Faith

Naomi Sharp

DEDICATION

I dedicate this book to Samantha Bell, as our journey together has been taken with footsteps of faith as we both watch our dreams come true, thank you for the honour of being your friend.

CONTENTS

1 Crossroads 1

2 Faith or Fear 27

3 The Setting Sun 62

4 Wishes in the Waterfalls 88

5 Lochs of Luck 115

6 Opening Pandora's Box 143

7 Footprints of Faith 170

8 About the Author 196

9 Other Books Written by Naomi Sharp 198

1 CROSSROADS

As Molly slowly lowered the letter to the table, the room filled with a deathly silence. The news of Molly's mum and dad returning back to the stars began to sink in. Hugh's gaze fixed on Molly. He did not know what to say to make things better, perhaps for the first time.

The silence was broken by the screech of Ben's chair as he slid it back along the floor and rose to his feet. He walked across the kitchen, flicked the switch on the kettle and moved towards Molly. 'May I?' he questioned gently, motioning towards the letter. Molly smiled meekly and nodded.

Ben sunk his left hand deep into the pocket of his jeans as he read through the letter. Molly slowly looked up and tilted her head back. 'What's going to happen to me, Ben?' she asked. She realised, in that moment, that everything she thought she knew was now unknown. Her future was now unwritten. Ben placed the letter back in front of Molly and turned to the now-boiling kettle. He didn't say a word.

Ben reached for a mug and put some coffee in. He poured the boiling water on top and watched it swirl around. He turned to Molly and Hugh. 'Please go and check that the horses in the barn have enough hay and water for the night.' Hugh and Molly looked at each other in disbelief but slowly got to their feet. They walked to the front door, slipped on their boots and coats, and stepped out onto the front porch in silence. They all listened and waited for the click of the front door closing.

Billy slid out one of the kitchen chairs and sat down at the table, clasping his hands together and placing them in front of him. Ben moved and sat opposite him. Ally flopped her head into her hands and ran her fingers through her hair. She shook her head, sadly. 'This can't be happening! This stuff doesn't happen in real life.' Billy reached across and gently took her hand.
'We have to figure out a plan for Molly,' he said carefully. 'She'll want answers when she steps back through that door.'

'Plan? What plan?' asked Ally in frustration. 'They were just here, having a cup of tea at this table! How can they be gone?' she exclaimed. Billy looked across at Ben. Ben took a sip of coffee, playing for time. He leant back in his chair as he watched tears trickle down Ally's cheeks.
'You'll have to go back to England with Molly to make arrangements. Does she have any other family?' Ben asked.

Ally's expression began to soften as she looked across at Ben. The realisation of the journey Molly was about to take became very real. She gently shook her head.
'The only family Molly had was Nana O,' Billy piped up. 'So, she will have to come and live with you two.'

Ally cautiously looked across at Ben. 'I bet this isn't quite what you bargained for when you first asked me and Hugh back to the ranch at the Country Fair and Rodeo?' she asked.
Ben reached across the table and took Ally's hand. 'Sometimes, the greatest love doesn't have the easiest start. There are tests which help a relationship to grow strong roots, like an old oak tree. So that, over time, when the tree has grown tall, it can withstand both the sunny and the stormy days with ease.'

Ally squeezed Ben's hand. 'Well, we sure are having our fair share of tests,' she said. She let go of Ben's hand and got up from the table. 'I best go and make that plan then,' she added with an obnoxious glare at Billy, before heading across into Ben's office. She closed the door loudly behind her, muttering to herself as she went. She was still getting used to Billy and his ways.

Just then, the front door opened and Molly and Hugh peered around the edge. 'Is it OK for us to come in?' Molly asked cautiously.
'Yes, of course,' Billy answered enthusiastically. He waved his hand and motioned for them to come and sit at the table.

Hugh and Molly took off their coats and boots, and made their way across to the table. Molly went and sat back down next to Billy. Billy put his arm around her, protectively. 'Are you OK?' he asked quietly. Molly mustered all her strength, forced a smile and nodded. Billy held her gaze. As he looked deep into her eyes, he could see the pain whirling around inside, like a raging, stormy sea.

Billy wrapped her in a hug and squeezed her tightly. 'We'll get through this,' he urged.
'Together, as a family,' he added with a whisper.

Molly untangled herself from his arms. 'I'm going to head upstairs for a little while,' she uttered, and slid off her chair. She shuffled her feet across the living room floor and used the banister to pull her body up the stairs. She felt herself grow heavier with each step.

Hugh watched Molly and felt an urgent yearning to fix everything. 'Maybe we could all sit down later and have a movie night together,' he suggested hopefully, still staring after Molly. 'That's a great idea,' confirmed Ben. 'But, don't forget, Molly needs to process the news. So, maybe give her a little time by herself,' he added. 'Yeah! She can have that alone-time whilst I get everything ready. That's long enough,' Hugh said, feeling his energy return. He bounced off his chair and ran upstairs to get his duvet.
Billy leant forwards and rested his elbows on the table. He looked across at Ben. 'So?' he asked, his tone hardening. 'Are you still happy with your decision? You're not just getting Ally, but Hugh too, and now perhaps Molly as well. Can the ranch support them all?' Billy asked with concern. Ben shuffled uncomfortably in his seat. 'Well, I've saved up my winnings. They should tie us over for a little while, whilst I make some changes,' he offered. 'But one thing is for sure, I will make it work,' he added with determination.

Billy settled back in his chair, sunk his hands into the pockets of his jeans and nodded. His eyes began to change as his thoughts gathered momentum. 'Well, I best be heading off,' he said as he was suddenly hit with the realisation of what he needed to do.

Billy reached across and picked up Molly's letter from Nana O. 'I'll take this up to Molly. I think she'll need all the hope she can get,' he said. He turned and made his way across the living room to where Hugh was now busy building a fire.

Hugh sensed Billy behind him as he placed the kindling carefully in the fire. 'Aren't you staying for movie night?' he asked, without turning around.

'Not tonight,' replied Billy. 'But, I'll be back tomorrow.'

'But this is family movie night, and we're family,' Hugh protested. He turned and placed his hands on his hips.

Billy abruptly stopped and looked down at Hugh. 'Umm, well,' he muttered uncomfortably. It had been a long while since he had done something as a family.

Hugh got up as Ben entered the room. 'I'm not asking, Grandpa Billy. You're staying for movie night. We need everyone to pull together to get through this,' Hugh asserted. Ben looked at Billy. 'I think you have met your match, Billy. Best do what the chief says! He can be pretty persistent when he gets an idea in his head,' Ben said with a smile, gesturing towards Hugh. Billy stood in shock. The silence seemed to stretch into forever. But he finally surrendered and nodded his agreement, before turning and heading to the stairs.

Billy made his way upstairs. His feet landed heavily on each step. He slowly pushed open Molly's door and found her curled up on her bed. Molly quickly squeezed her eyes shut as Billy silently moved across and laid the letter by her side. Even the darkness couldn't hide the tear stains on Molly's cheeks. Billy left the room as silently as he had entered it.

As Billy made his way back downstairs he could see that Hugh was already sitting on the couch with a bowl of popcorn. The fire was blazing enthusiastically in the background. Hugh turned around to look at Billy. 'Come on, Grandpa,' he invited, patting the space next to him.
Billy gingerly made his way across and sat down in the large chair next to the couch. 'This'll do just fine for me,' he said, as he lowered his tired body into the seat.

Ben was leaning against his office door, in deep conversation with Ally. Hugh and Billy could hear her ferociously tapping away at the computer keys. 'I'll drop you off in the morning,' Ben offered, before turning around and joining Hugh and Billy.

'Come on, Mom,' Hugh called with increasing restlessness. Ben came and sat down next to Hugh, pulling the duvet up over him. He placed his finger to his lips. 'It looks like it's going to be a lad's movie night,' observed Ben, as he pressed play on the DVD player.

Hugh was just about to object but Ben quickly intervened. He put his finger to his lips again, but more urgently this time, and pointed at the television: *keep quiet, Hugh*. In the background they could hear the printer working hard, as more and more paper was ejected. Ally scooped up the wodge of paper and briskly made her way out of the office and towards the stairs. She glanced at the three of them, now engrossed in the movie.

Ally made her way up the stairs. As she reached the top she could hear sniffling sounds coming from Molly's room, so she slowly pushed open the door. The landing light cast a soft glow over the objects in there. It illuminated the shape of Molly, curled up in a tight ball on her bed, shaking. Ally placed the paper on the end of the bed and quickly made her way over to her. She scooped Molly up in her arms and gently rocked her from side to side.

'I've got you,' Ally soothed. 'I will always be here,' she whispered, over and over again into Molly's ear.

Molly's tears finally began to slow down. She lifted her head and looked deep into Ally's eyes. 'I have just found a place called *Home*, and now I am going to lose it,' she sobbed. 'Ally, please don't make me go back! I want to stay here with you! I promise I won't be any trouble. I'll help out around the ranch. Please, Ally, don't make me go back,' she pleaded, as fresh tears began to tumble down her cheeks.

Ally squeezed Molly tightly, trying to fight back her own tears. As they stood at this seemingly impossible crossroads, she did not know the answer. After a long pause, Ally loosened her grip and looked back at Molly. 'I don't know what the future holds, Molly,' she declared honestly. 'But, tomorrow we need to fly back together and start to make some choices. With each decision we make and with each action we take, more of the path we need to go down will be revealed. But, for now, we just need to take that first step. We will slowly be able to see what is ahead,' Ally said lovingly. 'We will be leaving in the morning, so I need you to pack your suitcase tonight.' Ally began to move away and reached for the papers. Molly quickly grabbed hold of Ally's arm. 'Please, Ally! If I leave, I may never be able to come back! Please, Ally. I want to stay at home. This is my home!' Molly said urgently as she rose to her knees.

Ally felt her heart tear apart as she looked at Molly in despair. She couldn't watch the pain anymore. She quickly made her way to the door, holding the pile of papers tightly to her beating chest. 'I'll bring your suitcase downstairs later,' Ally said quickly, before making her way towards her own bedroom.

Molly's head sunk lower and lower as the pain crumbled every cell of her body into desperation. 'Please let me stay at home,' she whispered, trying desperately to soothe herself. She became tormented by the stark realisation that, never again, would she be able to tell her mum and dad that she loved them. Never again would she be wrapped in the protection of their arms. Never again would she receive a kiss goodnight from them.

Molly's body began to tremble, uncontrollably. The life that was in her was shaken to its very core. She reached for the letter from Nana O that was still laying on the bottom of the bed, where Billy had left it. She lowered herself back onto the pillows and curled up into a tight, protective ball. She gently rocked and tried to gasp for air as her body began to shut down.

Ally walked slowly down the landing towards her room. She switched on the light and rested her head against the wall: *How am I going to get through this?* She trudged her way to the wardrobe, opened it up and pulled out her suitcase. She dropped it heavily onto the bed.

Ally's eyes glazed over as the reality of it all engulfed her. Never in a million years did she think she would be going back to England for these reasons.

'Sometimes things have to fall apart before they can be put back together again in a new way,' a voice said. Ally looked up to see Ben standing in the doorway. He glided across the room, wrapped her in a hug and kissed her on the cheek.

Ally's arms automatically gripped onto Ben's body. 'This doesn't feel like my world is falling apart,' she answered sadly. 'This feels like my world is crashing apart.' She let out a deep sigh and Ben squeezed her tighter. But, she slowly began to feel that familiar feeling that seemed to take hold whenever she was in Ben's arms. The love was re-awoken inside of her and the room grew just a little bit brighter.

'It feels like life is repeating itself again,' Ally muffled into Ben's chest. 'I thought all that stuff with Hugh's dad dying was done. But, this all seems to be waking up a sleeping dragon inside of me.'

Ben began to smile as he peeled Ally from his body. 'It will always be part of your story, Ally,' he replied. 'But it doesn't need to dictate your future choices,' he added as he guided her to sit on the bed. He knelt on one knee in front of her. 'This time you don't have to go through this alone,' he said lovingly, as he gently played with Ally's engagement ring between his fingers.

Ally glanced down and couldn't stop a smile creeping out as she looked deep into Ben's eyes. She slowly recognised a sparkle, a light deep inside that shone so bright.

'It takes great faith to love,' said Ben. 'Because, where there is love, there will be loss,' he added. His forehead wrinkled with concentration. 'The alternative is to never love at all. But, then there would be no opportunity to experience one of the greatest achievements of mankind.'

Ally placed a hand on each of Ben's shoulders. 'You know, sometimes, I do wonder were these wise words come from,' she said bewildered, but slightly bemused.

Ben lifted his hand and pointed to Ally's heart. 'Listen to the whispers of wisdom from deep within, for that is where the answers to life are, and the steps that need to be taken.'

Ally excitedly flung her arms around Ben's neck, causing him to lose his balance. They both started to chuckle. 'Even in the darkest hour, you bring light, laughter and love,' Ally said with heartfelt admiration.

'That's because all of those things are the cement that is holding our new life together. Now, come on, Miss Ally. This suitcase won't pack itself.'

Ally playfully flopped back onto the bed in protest. But she soon erupted into a belly-roaring laugh as she felt Ben's fingers begin to tickle her. 'Stop! Stop!' Ally gasped. 'OK, I'll pack,' she managed to stutter between giggles.

Ally crawled off the bed and walked across to the wardrobe. She pulled out her clothes and passed them to Ben. He folded them and placed them in the suitcase. They were suddenly interrupted by the sound of the door creaking. Ben looked up to see Molly standing there. She looked so lost. He sunk back down onto his knees and opened his arms wide. Molly scurried across to him and snuggled gratefully into his chest. She buried herself into the safety of his arms.

'How are you getting on with your packing?' Ben whispered tentatively. He felt a slight shake of Molly's head in response. 'Would you like some help?' he asked gently. Molly's fingers tightened their grip on Ben's shirt. Ben looked up and watched Ally disappear into the bathroom. She glanced down at him as she passed and gave him a weak smile. Ben casually scooped Molly up into his arms and began to carry her through to her bedroom.

Ben glanced over the landing-balcony to see Billy and Hugh, both fast asleep, as the ending credits of the film serenaded them. He continued to walk with Molly into her room, flicking the light switch on as he entered. He placed Molly carefully on the bed. 'Now, how about we do this together?' he asked as he reached under the bed to pull out Molly's suitcase.

Molly sat, unmoving, like a statue. She watched Ben cautiously as he began to move around the room, placing her clothes back into the suitcase. 'I will be able to come back, won't I?' Molly muttered under her breath.
Ben paused a moment and looked across at Molly. 'You can always come back, whenever you want. There will always be a home for you here,'

he reassured her with conviction, before taking a jumper and placing it in the suitcase.

Molly felt a welcome wave of relief wash over her as she grasped onto this piece of hope. Ben placed the last piece of clothing into the suitcase. He was just about to close the lid when Molly quickly slipped the note from Nana O on top of her clothes. She listened as the zip whizzed around the case. That was it. It was done. She was leaving. Ben lifted the suitcase onto the floor. 'Come on, you. I think you better get some sleep. Tomorrow is going to be a long day,' Ben said, as he rolled back the duvet. Molly climbed under and moved her pillow to the other end of the bed so she could look out of the window. Ben pulled the duvet up around her and tucked her in.

Ben reached across to turn off the light. The room descended into darkness and the sky became illuminated by the stars. He shuffled down and lay next to Molly, and they both stared silently out at the night sky. Molly carefully lifted her hand and pointed at three stars, all in a row. 'There is mum, dad and Nana O,' she said quietly. They both gazed at the three stars sparkling in the sky. Words were not needed in that moment. Ben eventually heard Molly's breathing deepen and slow. He was thankful to see that exhaustion had finally got the better of her. It was too much.

Ben carefully slid off the bed and crept out of the room. He made sure a thin crack of light from the landing could make its way into Molly's room, before slowly making his way down the stairs to his office. As he passed Hugh and Billy, he reached over for the TV remote and switched it off. He then walked into the kitchen to make himself a much-needed cup of coffee, before escaping into the solitude of his office. He carefully closed the door so as not to wake anyone. He placed his coffee on the desk and flopped heavily into his chair. His head fell into his hands and he surrendered to his tears as they finally escaped.

Everything became still as Ben's body shook and the tears streamed down his cheeks. He didn't notice Ally open the door and walk across to perch on the edge of his desk. He suddenly felt her presence and lifted his head out of his hands. He quickly shot back in his chair and self-consciously tried to wipe away any evidence of his tears. Ally shook her head, leant forwards and wrapped her arms reassuringly around him. He realised that he had no choice but to allow her to comfort him and he felt his body begin to relax again.

'There is no shame in sharing tears,' Ally whispered reassuringly as she gently rocked Ben from side to side.

Ben let out a large sigh and brought his head away from Ally's body. 'I guess,' he stuttered. Ally took Ben's hand and began to guide him back out of the office. 'It's been a long day for all of us,' Ally confirmed as she switched off the lights.

'Where's Hugh?' Ben asked as they walked past the now-empty sofa and chair.

'I carried Hugh to bed,' answered Ally. 'And Billy is sleeping in the guest room,' she added. She tugged at Ben's hand and they climbed the stairs together, their footsteps the only sound in the house. They reached the bedroom, changed into their pyjamas and slid gratefully under the duvet. Ally snuggled up to Ben and rested her head on his chest. Ben wrapped his arms around Ally's body. 'Quite a day, huh?' said Ben as he stared up at the ceiling.

'Just another bend in the river of life,' Ally managed to whisper before the welcome relief of sleep took over.

BANG!!

Ben shot bolt upright in bed as the noise from downstairs echoed through the house. He squinted as his eyes tried to readjust to the morning light. He felt groggy and disorientated.

Once he had got his bearings, he whipped back the duvet and briskly made his way down the stairs to investigate the noise. As he approached the kitchen he saw a frozen Billy, holding a frying pan in mid-air, Molly covered in flour and Hugh pointing at a spatula. Ben stopped to take in the scene before him. 'Morning,' he croaked as he shook his head. He walked across to the kettle to make himself a coffee, and Ally, a cup of tea.

The three of them stood, like statues, whilst they watched Ben move around the kitchen and then disappear back upstairs. Billy crept over to the edge of the kitchen and slowly peered around the corner. When he was happy that Ben had reached the landing and was out of ear shot, he spun around. 'Right. So, here is the plan,' he said, as he marched over to the cooker and put the frying pan down.

Hugh came up behind with the pancake mixture. All three of them watched him pour it into the pan and listened to the sizzling sounds of it cooking. 'Tom should be here in the next hour,' confirmed Billy. 'Molly, when he arrives, could you make him a coffee? Then you two head out and complete morning chores, whilst I tell Ben.'

'You know he really isn't going to like this plan,' Molly asserted as she began to set the table.

Billy slowly turned around and leant against the worktop. 'I know. But Ben has had to do this all by himself for far too long. He didn't have anyone he could turn to. He has become a great man because of it. Not many people you meet can lead others with love, and inspiration to be their best,' he explained. 'But, things are different now. Ben needs to realise that he has people around him who want to help, and are more than ready to put into practice all the skills he has helped to nurture in them.'

Hugh carefully carried the frying pan over to the plates and tipped the first pancake out. He then returned back to the cooker to begin the next one. They heard footsteps coming back down the stairs. They listened carefully, glanced at each other and smiled. Billy placed his hand in the centre of the room, Molly put her hand on top and then Hugh added his to the hand-pile. 'Ready?' asked Billy excitedly.
'Ready!' Hugh and Molly chuckled in unison.

Ben walked across the living room and placed Ally's suitcase by the front door. His heart began to hurt. He never wanted to see this suitcase again, not for a long while, at least. He let out an audible sigh as he dragged his feet to the kitchen. He took a huge gulp of air, straightened up, forced a smile and went to sit at the table.

Hugh scurried across and placed a pancake on Ben's plate in front of him. Molly followed swiftly behind and brought fresh coffee. 'I'll take over,' Billy said as he motioned for Hugh to go and have his breakfast too. Molly glanced up at Billy and he nodded for her to do the same. As they each took their places, they heard Ally's footsteps tread along the landing and then down the stairs.

They were tucking into their pancakes as Ally arrived in the kitchen. She pulled up a chair next to Molly. Her eyes were red from the morning's tears. Ben looked at her and another sharp pain shot through his heart: *How could he protect her whilst she was away?*
Billy swiftly came across and placed a pancake in front of Ally. He laid an encouraging hand gently on her shoulder as he passed. Just then, he glanced out the window and saw Tom's truck turn down the driveway. He managed to catch Hugh's attention with a quick raise of his eyebrows, signalling that it was time for them to head outside.

Hugh nudged Molly under the table and she scowled back at him, not comprehending. He glared back, more urgently this time. 'Ooh,' uttered Molly as she slowly deciphered his gestures. She placed the final piece of pancake in her mouth, and Hugh quickly collected the plates and placed them by the sink. He took hold of Molly's hand and dragged her to the front door. 'Just off to do morning chores,' Hugh called over his shoulder, as he and Molly grabbed their boots and coats. Within a flash, they were out the front door.

Ally stared at the pancake in front of her. Her stomach tried to rumble a '*yes please*' but she held her breath and pushed the plate away. 'I'll be in the office making calls if you need me,' she said. She got to her feet and pulled her cardigan tightly around her body. She walked across to the office and quickly closed the door behind her. Molly and Hugh were on the front porch, pulling on their boots and coats as Tom's truck pulled up outside the house. He stepped out and called a cheery '*morning*' at them. He gave a cheeky grin and tipped his hat as he bounded up to the front door. Molly and Hugh both broke into a sprint in the opposite direction, towards the barn.

Tom walked through the front door, took off his hat and scanned the room. 'Morning, Tom,' called Billy from the kitchen. Tom turned to see Billy and Ben sitting at the kitchen table. 'Fresh coffee in the pot,' Billy added casually. Tom glanced at Billy to try and figure out how much had been disclosed. He took Ben's relatively calm manner to mean that he must not know yet.

Tom briskly walked past Ben, placed his hat on the table and poured himself a cup of coffee. 'Is everything alright?' Ben asked, breaking the silence. Tom sheepishly joined them at the table and looked directly at Billy. Ben glanced quizzically across at both of them. 'Well, at some point,' he said. 'Someone is going to enlighten me as to what you are both up to.'

'Tom's good at talking,' answered Billy with a cheeky smile. 'I think I'll let him explain,' he added.
'Ha! I don't think so, Billy,' countered Tom. 'It was your idea, so I think you should be the one to tell Ben.'
Billy readjusted himself in his seat, leant forwards on the table and looked at Ben. 'I called Tom up last night and explained the situation, told him what has happened,' Billy began. 'We were both in agreement that if you had someone to look after the ranch, then you would be going with Ally.'

Ben remained silent as he absorbed Billy's words. Tom stepped in at this point and continued. 'You know I will always have your back, Ben,' he reassured. 'So, I have come to help Billy and we're going to run the ranch while you are away.' Ben leant back in his chair and took in a deep, steadying breath. But, Billy interjected before Ben could speak. 'There is a plane ticket for you and one for Hugh, waiting for you both at the airport. I called in a favour with a friend,' Billy continued. 'Chad will be joining us in a few days too. I called him this morning,' Tom finished.

Ben took in another deep breath and tried to push down the tears of gratitude that were rapidly forming in his throat. He coughed in an attempt to clear them and looked down at the wood-grain in the kitchen table. He couldn't think what to say. 'Thank you,' he finally muttered as he headed off upstairs to pack.

Tom and Billy remained at the kitchen table, a little stunned. 'That wasn't quite how that was supposed to go,' Tom said in amazement. 'Wasn't he meant to kick off, like he normally does, and ramble on about how he couldn't possibly leave the ranch? But, all we got was that *thank you*,' he added.
Billy looked at Tom with concern in his eyes. 'He is not in good shape,' he said gravely. 'And the journey ahead is going to be tough.' He interlocked his fingers in front of him, lost in his own thoughts.

'What's going to happen with Ally, Hugh and Molly?' asked Tom. 'Are they going to still live here? Is the engagement off? What is Ben going to do with the ranch?' Tom continued to reel off the questions but all Billy could do was shrug his shoulders. Eventually they both fell silent.

The silence was eventually broken by the sound of Hugh and Molly racing back from the barn to the front porch. 'I won,' chimed Molly as she stood, breathless at the door, with her arms held up in celebration. They came bustling into the kitchen, taking off their boots and coats as they did so.
'So?' questioned Hugh excitedly. 'How did it go, Grandpa?' he asked as he bounced towards Billy.
'Well, we have the green light, kids. Best roll out Phase Two,' confirmed Billy.
Hugh ran across to Molly, picked her up and swung her around.
'Yay!' Hugh cried with a huge beaming smile.

'OK! OK!' Molly shouted. She patted Hugh on the shoulders. 'Put me down before I throw up,' she added dramatically. Hugh quickly put Molly down and stepped back, keen to get out of the firing line. Molly stopped a moment and they all watched as a smile began to spread across her face. 'Come on, Hugh,' she instructed. 'Let's get our stuff before they come back down.' Molly grabbed Hugh's hand and dragged him up the stairs.

They both raced to the top of the stairs and ran to their rooms. Just moments later they were pulling their suitcases back down. The cases bumped repetitively but enthusiastically against each step. They were wheeling them across to the front door, but abruptly stopped as they heard the office door open. 'What is that noise?' Ally asked angrily. Molly and Hugh froze behind their suitcases, unsure about what to say. But Ben suddenly appeared with his suitcase. He placed it down next to Molly's to join the line-up. 'What's happening?' asked Ally in confusion.
'We're going to be late if we don't hit the highway soon,' Ben said cheekily with a smirk.
'We?' repeated Ally as the pieces of the puzzle started to fit together.

'But...but,' Ally stuttered. At that moment Tom got up from the kitchen table and placed his hat back on his head.
'Morning, Miss Ally,' he said as he walked past her and headed back outside.
'Mom! Come on! We'll explain on the way!' Hugh exclaimed, jumping up and down on the spot.
'Let's go,' he added as he took hold of his suitcase handle and dragged it out onto the front

porch. He was followed closely by Molly and Ben.

Ally's look turned to ice as she glared at Billy. Billy quickly scooted out of his seat. 'I'll start up the truck,' he said before disappearing outside. He nearly crashed into Ben as he scurried away. Ben reappeared and took hold of Ally's suitcase and handbag. 'We are going to do this as a family,' he explained lovingly. 'Tom and Billy are going to look after the ranch, and I am going to try and survive meeting my mother-in-law to be,' he continued. Ally's face turned from thunder to fear at the thought.

'I'll explain the rest on the way,' Ben said and he motioned for Ally to follow. Ally snapped out of her daze, took one last look around her new, beautiful home and grabbed her coat. She stepped bravely outside and closed the door behind her. 'I can do this,' she said determinedly. She closed her eyes and dug deep within herself to find her strength. She finally took a deep breath and joined everyone in the truck. With a final slam of all the doors, they set off for the airport.

2 FAITH OR FEAR

Ally finally led Hugh, Molly and Ben down the steps of the plane and onto English ground. They were greeted by a brisk wind which whirled relentlessly around them. Ally pulled her coat more tightly around her body. 'Brrr,' she shivered. 'Why does it always feel so much colder here?' she mumbled.

 'Because of the moisture content, Mom,' explained Hugh. 'It's a lot damper here than where we have come from,' he added. Ally just shivered in response.

They followed the throng of people into Arrivals and towards Baggage Claim. Ben suddenly felt a little hand take hold of his. He looked down to see Molly by his side, but his curiosity quickly turned into concern as he saw the colour begin to drain from her face. He gave her hand a little, reassuring squeeze as they proceeded through security and into the baggage hall. Ben remained quiet as he scanned the airport. He had never felt so far out of his comfort zone before.

'Everything alright?' inquired Ally as she watched Ben turn the same shade of white as Molly. She looked him up and down. He had swapped his cowboy hat for a baseball hat, jeans and t-shirt. Ben snapped out of his daze and offered Ally a weak smile, but before she could ask anymore, the conveyor belt started up and their suitcases tumbled into view.

'I've got this,' Ben said. He placed his hand on Ally's shoulder and began to pull each of their suitcases over. Molly followed his every move, like a loyal shadow.
Ally and Hugh were watching Molly and Ben. 'I would say it's going to all be alright,' said Hugh with worry in his eyes. 'But I'm not that sure.'
'Well, let's try and make this the best trip that we can,' replied Ally. 'Maybe it's time for you to work your magic with a map again,' she added with a sparkle in her eye.

Hugh's eyes lit up with excitement as Ally handed him some money. 'Back in a minute,' he said as he darted off into the crowd. Ben pulled the last of the suitcases off and dragged it behind him. The weight felt like the burden he was already carrying. Ally continued to watch Hugh's head as he weaved his way through the crowds, towards the information desk.

Hugh reached the desk, stood on his tip-toes and peered over the edge. 'Hello?' he called, glancing from side to side. There was no response.
'Excuse me! Anyone there?' he enquired further, a little more loudly this time. A lady suddenly appeared out of a doorway. She had bright, crimson lips and was dressed in an incredibly smart uniform.
'Hello,' she said politely. 'How can I help?' She took her place at the desk-computer and began tapping away at the keys, but without looking at Hugh.
Hugh tilted his head in confusion at her behaviour. 'I would like a map of England please, Miss,' he answered.
The lady slid open a draw by her side, took out a map and passed it to Hugh. Still, she did not take her eyes off the computer screen. 'Is there anything else?' she said rudely.

Hugh lowered himself back down and took a step back from the desk. 'No. That is all, thank you,' he said, feeling a little dejected.
'Excuse me, young man,' said a familiar voice

behind him. Hugh spun around.

'Jane!' he shouted as he stuffed the map in his pocket and flung his arms around her. He squeezed her tightly.

'Hello, traveller,' Jane replied, squeezing him back. Hugh grabbed her hand and they ran back towards where Ally, Ben and Molly were waiting. Ally anxiously scanned the crowds, but soon heard Hugh's voice. 'Mom, Mom, Mom!' he shouted.

'I'm here!' Ally answered, with obvious relief. She turned and saw Hugh running towards her, weaving his way through the crowds. But, he had a lady with him. As her eyes adjusted, Ally suddenly lit up with delight. 'Jane!' she cried with outstretched arms. The two women embraced as they reached each other.

'Boy, have I missed you,' Jane said and hugged Ally tightly. Jane stepped back and scanned Ally up and down. 'Whatever you are on, I want some! You look amazing!' she declared with open admiration.

Ally shuffled a little self-consciously, unable to hold back her smile. 'Love works wonders,' she mumbled shyly.

'Jane, this is Ben,' Hugh interrupted with raised eyebrows.

Jane took a step towards Ben. 'Well, that would do it,' she said as she shook his hand warmly.

'Nice to meet you, Mam,' Ben replied, politely taking off his hat.

This was all a little bit too much for Molly. She began to feel increasingly agitated with everyone and she slammed her hand down on her suitcase handle. She proceeded to drag it across to the doors, but suddenly stopped. The fight was gone. She watched the rain drops slowly roll down the window, mirroring the tears that she was desperately holding inside.

Hugh's reflection began to come into focus alongside her. He reached down and took her hand. 'You won't be going through this on your own,' he asserted reassuringly. 'We may not have the same parents, but I am your brother now, which means we stick together, no matter what,' he added as he stared determinedly into Molly's eyes.

'The car is this way,' Jane said as she glided past them both and pushed the door open. Molly kept hold of Hugh's hand as they all made their way to the car. There was a frantic few minutes of suitcase-loading and seat-finding, but they were soon on their way to Ally's house. Ally and Jane's constant, happy chatter filled the car during the journey. Hugh, Ben and Molly all took this time to sit quietly in the back and watch the countryside roll by.

Jane's car soon pulled up outside the front door of Ally's house. She turned off the ignition and the car suddenly became silent. Why did silence sometimes sound so loud? Ally fell into a daze as she stared at her front door. She was catapulted back to the day she stepped over the threshold. The day she walked away from her past and into an unwritten future, full of dreams and the illusion of uncertainty. She felt a hand on her shoulder. It was Jane. 'A lot has happened since you stepped out that front door,' said Jane. 'Who would have known what was waiting for you, just down the road. I don't think either of us could have guessed that you would transform into the person you are today.'

Ally leant across and placed her head on Jane's shoulder. 'It would have been a lot easier if life had given me a bit of a heads up,' she chuckled.

'Ah now, where is the fun in that?' Jane replied with a smile. 'You needed to prove to you that your faith in yourself was stronger than your fears. You wouldn't have remembered the strength inside if not. And the fire of fight that is now burning bright,' she added.

'I hear you,' Ally said. She sat back up, unclipped her belt and stepped out into the rain. She carefully opened up the front door. It was her house but she felt like she was looking at a place that she didn't know.

Ally walked slowly into the living room. It looked like a time capsule of a chapter that had long been forgotten. Ally was followed by Hugh, who ran straight up to his room. Back in the car, Ben reached for the door handle as Jane turned around in her seat to look at him. 'Thank you doesn't seem big enough for what you have done for Ally and Hugh,' she said with sincerity. 'But, we can all plainly see Ally's transformation into a women we never thought we would see again,' she added gratefully.

Ben smiled. 'I didn't stand a chance,' he said teasingly. 'When I met her, my heart made its decision there and then. Nothing I could do to stop it. Sometimes life offers us the opportunity to experience a love so pure and unconditional,' he added wisely. 'I think Ally has helped me more than I have helped her.' With that, he stepped out and walked into the house.

Jane then turned to look at Molly. 'Now, you must be Molly,' she said with a cheeky smile. Molly nodded her head shyly. 'And your parents have died. Is that correct?' she asked directly.

Molly's expression instantly turned to thunder. 'Yes. But you don't have to be so blunt about it,' she retaliated.

Jane's smile remained. 'A fact is a fact,' she stated matter-of-factly. 'It doesn't make it any less or more of a moment in time. It's our emotions that do that. They dictate the influence that each moment is going to have on our future,' she added. 'You have a choice now. What seeds are you going to plant for your future?' she directed at Molly, but left the question hanging. 'When Ally left this house, she didn't know what was ahead of her. She just knew her future wasn't in this house and that the life she was leading wasn't what she wanted. So, she made a bold move and took a leap of faith. She could have stayed and continued to play out her old story, but instead, she turned the page and started to re-write it. What is it that you want?' Jane finished wisely.

Molly's look began to soften. 'I want a place I can call home. A place that is filled with love, laughter and all the good things in life,' she answered as she wiggled her toes.
'Very well then,' said Jane. 'Are you prepared to take the journey? Are you ready to pull out all the weeds of old beliefs, and plant new flowers?' she continued.
Molly shuffled in her seat, unsure for a moment, but then sat up tall. 'Yes I am!' she declared with conviction.
'Well, OK then,' answered Jane. 'You best go and join the others,' she added with a sparkle in her

eyes. Molly stared intently. She had seen that look once before. She began to sift through her memories, in search of why it was so familiar. That was it! That was the same look Nana O had given her the day she left the cottage, the day she had learnt about following her…

Molly suddenly burst into life. 'Nana O!' she cried. 'Follow my intuition. It will guide me through this,' she shouted. Jane calmly stepped out of the car. As she passed Molly's window, she gave her a wink of acknowledgement. Molly felt her strength begin to build. It was like her very own star in her belly, starting to shine brighter and brighter. She leaped out of the car and took her suitcase inside. With a final turn, she closed the front door and shut the world out for the night.

***

As the morning sunlight shone through the window, Ally's eyelids began to flicker. She instinctively put out her hand. Instead of the empty bed she had felt months before, her fingers now felt the warmth of Ben's skin and the rhythm of his heartbeat, as his chest gently rose and fell. A smile shot across her face. She jumped up onto her feet and bounced up and down on the bed, like a child. 'Good morning, everyone!' she yelled at the top of her lungs.

The bedroom door suddenly swung open and Hugh and Molly darted in. They joined Ally in her antics. 'Wakey-wakey, Sleepy-head!' they shouted in unison as they bounced around Ben. A very sleepy Ben reached up to tickle his human alarm clocks, and the house started to fill with the joyous sounds of belly roaring laughs and squeals.

A few minutes later the noise began to subside and they all lay on the bed at different angles. 'Line up, troops!' Ally ordered with a smile as she jumped off the bed. Ben, Hugh and Molly sniggered and moved to the end of the bed. 'Today is an important day,' Ally stated. 'We will have to work together to get through this as quickly and easily as possible,' she said, parading up and down. 'Ben!' she said.

'Yes, Mam,' replied Ben with a shout, and a salute.

'You're in charge of food,' Ally instructed.

'Yes, Mam!' he confirmed as he grabbed his clothes and headed downstairs to start breakfast.

'And you, young man,' Ally directed at Hugh.

'Yes, Mam?' Hugh said, copying Ben.

'You are in charge of our to-do list and organising the billions of pieces of paper we are going to get today,' she continued.

'On it like a sonnet,' Hugh affirmed before he

disappeared into his room to find his old school exercise book and an empty folder.

'And you, young lady,' Ally said, softening her voice and kneeling down in front of Molly. 'You are going to have to be brave and courageous. You are going to be asked millions of questions. Just answer them honestly and tell the truth about what you want.'

'I promise,' said Molly as she placed her hands on her hips, like Wonder Woman.

Just then, the doorbell rang, interrupting Ally and Molly. They listened as Ben made his way to the door and opened it. 'Morning, Jane,' Ben greeted as he stepped aside to let her in.

Jane pulled a face of uncertainty. 'Are you ready for today?' she asked tentatively.

'I don't think you could ever be ready for a day like today,' Ben replied gravely as he closed the door. 'Come on through, Jane. I've just put some coffee on,' he said, trying to lighten the moment.

Hugh came bounding down the stairs and flew past Jane. 'Woah, where's the fire?' Jane asked with a chuckle.

'Deep in here,' Hugh said with a glint of mischief in his eyes, as he pointed to his stomach.

'What are you up to, young man?' Jane asked, recognising that look. But, Hugh quickly disappeared into the living room. Ally then appeared in the kitchen, followed closely by Molly. 'He's even house trained,' Jane said amiably, gesturing towards Ben as she took the welcome cup of coffee from him. 'Do you think he could teach my man back home? I've tried for decades,' she added with mock drama. Ally simply smiled and walked across to give Ben a proud kiss on the cheek.

Molly began to feel increasingly uncomfortable as she stood and observed the three of them. 'I think I'll go and check on what Hugh is up to,' she said, trying to find any excuse to leave. They all watched her walk into the living room.

When Jane was sure Molly was out of ear-shot, she seized the moment. 'So, what's the plan?' she asked with impatience.

Ally took a seat at the kitchen table and gratefully accepted a plate of freshly made toast from Ben. 'Well, we'll have to head back to Molly's house first,' she answered. 'We're going to be met by the attorney there, who will read the wills. Then we will have to go to the estate agents. And then Molly will want to revisit Nana O's place, I assume.' Ally's shoulders began to slump. The weight of the day already felt too heavy to carry.

Jane pulled out a chair and sat down, opposite

Ally. 'Do you know who is going to have Molly?' she asked cautiously. Ben promptly joined them at the table and took hold of Ally's hand.

'We are,' Ben confirmed. He glanced down and suddenly noticed that Ally had removed her engagement ring. His gaze began to harden slightly. 'Lost something?' he inquired.

Ally froze. 'No! No, I just didn't think it was the right time, you know, with all that we have got to get through today,' she answered. For the first time, Ben's body crippled with the pain of disappointment inside.

Ally saw the hurt in Ben's eyes. She placed her hand in her pocket, took out her ring and slid it back on her finger. She placed her hand back on top of Ben's and smiled sincerely. Jane lifted up her cup and tried to look casual but, try as she might, she could not hide her beaming smile. Ally playfully tapped Jane on the arm. 'Oh, don't give me that look. Go on, say it,' she said with a playful sigh.

Jane quickly placed her cup down on the table and scooped them both up into her arms. 'Agh!!!' she cried. 'I am so happy for you guys! This is amazing news!'

Hugh and Molly ran back into the kitchen, keen to see what all the commotion was about. 'Oh, that's old news,' Hugh said dismissively and promptly sauntered back into the living room. But, Molly stayed and gazed at the ring. It sparkled keenly in the light and her expression began to change from confusion to determination. In that moment, she knew exactly what she wanted, and nothing was going to stop her from receiving it.

'Right,' announced Jane. 'I'll start the car up.' She made her way to the front door, with Hugh hot on her heels.
'Molly?' asked Ben gently, pulling her out of her thoughts. 'Are you alright?'
'Yep,' Molly answered quickly as she spun on her heels and marched out to the car. Ally turned to Ben and she placed her hand tenderly on his cheek. Ben closed his eyes momentarily. 'I love you so much,' she said softly, before sealing her words with a kiss.

Ben opened his eyes and felt a surge of love rise up from deep inside. 'Let's go and take the action needed to make our family's dreams come true,' he said boldly as he got up and headed out to the car. Ally's mind flashed back to the day she had sat on this very floor in a heap of tears. She let out a sigh and shook away the memory before making her way there too.

Jane pushed down harder on the accelerator as she weaved in and out of the cars. Ben's grip tightened on the car door handle, turning his knuckles white. Molly tapped her feet impatiently on the floor. Her focus narrowed like a laser beam as they drove down the road towards her house. Jane pulled up onto the driveway and the car descended into silence once more. They all sat and stared at the house. Molly reached into her pocket and pulled out the house key. Her hands shook momentarily. 'Well, there is no point us all sitting here,' she said bravely. 'Let's get the job done,' she added as she opened her car door and stepped out. Hugh slid out of the car as well. The adults watched the two of them slowly approach the front door.

Molly held the key up towards the door but found she couldn't go any further. Hugh placed his hand over hers, took the key from her and turned it in the lock. They listened to the click and then the door began to swing open. Hugh stepped inside. The house seemed like it was frozen in time. Nothing had changed from the moment they had left. He bent down and picked up the pile of post, walked into the kitchen and placed it on the table.

A cold shiver ran down Molly's spine. Maybe this wasn't going to be as easy as she thought it was going to be. She took a deep breath, reached inside and took hold of the garage key. 'Hugh!' she cried, her voice ringing around the empty house. 'I need you.' Hugh reappeared at the kitchen doorway and they both stepped outside. 'We need to get out the spare boxes that my dad was saving,' explained Molly. 'The ones that were for packing up Nana O's house that we didn't end up using,' she continued.

'I'll be with you in just a moment,' Hugh said as he dashed out to the car.

Jane wound down the window. 'That bad?' Ally said as she looked at Hugh's concerned face.

'Well, put it this way,' said Hugh. 'Yorkshire tea shares are definitely going to go up this week,' he added with a chuckle. He headed back to the house and traced Molly's footsteps into the garage. Ally looked once more at the house and watched Molly and Hugh begin to bring empty boxes inside. 'Right,' she said to Ben and Jane with determination. 'Could you pop to the shops and get us some tea, milk, biscuits, bin liners and something for lunch please? I have a feeling we are going to be here all day,' she declared as she stepped out of the car.

Ally walked into the house as Jane's car screeched off. She scanned the space and suddenly felt so overwhelmed. She slid her coat off in resignation and hung it on the banister. 'I think we should wait until the attorney arrives to read the will,' Ally called in an attempt to locate Molly and Hugh.

Molly came powering past her from the kitchen, holding a box. 'No, I am going to pack up my room. I want to put aside all the things I want to keep before they arrive,' she said with determination. 'Hugh!' she shouted. Hugh rushed through with an empty box and jumped up the stairs, two at a time.

Molly looked coldly at Ally who remained motionless in the hallway. She followed Hugh and stepped into her room. As she looked around she no longer felt anything towards her belongings. They were just things. It was the memories she wanted to box up instead. She stood up tall and reached for the blanket that Nana O had made her and placed it in the box. She then knelt down and slid out the tea set that had also been given to her, and put that in the box too. 'Do you have the bin liners?' Molly asked Hugh. The adrenaline began to wear off and her body ached.

Hugh reached into one of the boxes and lifted out a black roll of bin bags. Molly rolled up her duvet and stuffed it into a bag. Hugh did the same with the pillows. 'They can go to the charity shop,' Molly whispered. She slid a chair heavily across to the window and began to take down the curtains. She flung them on the floor as the anger began to reappear. 'These too,' she said bitterly. Her footsteps hardened as she marched across the floor to the wardrobe, and began to rip her clothes off the hangers. She threw them aggressively onto a fast growing pile. 'And these!' she cried. Hugh quickly shoved them into the bin liners. He ran up and down the stairs and made a pile of full bags outside the house.

Hugh was just putting out the next bag when Jane and Ben arrived back. Ben stepped out of the car with a shopping bag. Hugh puffed the words *'charity shop'* before dashing back into the house again. Ben walked past as Jane got out and began to load up the car with the bin bags. 'Ally?' Ben shouted.
'In here,' Ally replied. Ben watched Hugh run up and down the stairs with yet more bin liners before following Ally's voice into the living room.

Ben looked at Ally. She was sitting on the sofa with a book in front of her. He put the bag of shopping down, sat by her side and wrapped his arm around her waist. Ally wiped away a tear and smiled meekly. 'It's a book with a photo of them all, and there are sayings,' she explained as she began to turn the pages.
An idea suddenly dawned on Ben. 'Is there a

printer around here?' he asked.

Ally glanced up, confused. 'Yeah,' she confirmed. 'In that cupboard over there,' she said. Ben went over to the cupboard Ally was pointing at, opened the door and turned on the printer.

'Right,' said Jane. 'That's the first load. I'm going to head off to the charity shop,' she announced. Ally looked round. 'What are you on about, Jane?' she queried.

Jane raised her eyebrows. 'Have you not seen the tornado that is currently spinning around every room?' she asked.

Ally jumped to her feet and ran up the stairs. She peered into Molly's room and found that it was completely bare, except for one solitary box in the centre. It had the words, *Molly's Room* written on the top. Ally was suddenly brought back to reality by a banging noise. She ran towards it and stood in the next doorway. Hugh pushed by her with another black bag. Ally stepped inside the room. 'Molly, what are you doing?' she asked in shock. Molly appeared out of the wardrobe and threw yet more bundles of clothes onto the floor. 'Getting the house ready to be sold,' she said robotically as she turned to grab another pile.

Ally knelt down and let her fingers run over the fabric. She closed her eyes. 'Don't you want to hold onto to them for a little while?' she whispered through the piercing pain. She slowly opened her eyes and looked at Molly.

Molly paused. 'Why would I want to hold onto the past?' she replied. 'They aren't going to use them again. And neither am I. But there is someone out there who could really use all this stuff,' she continued innocently.

Ben stood at the bottom of the stairs and listened to the conversation between Molly and Ally. He was holding a picture in his hand. 'Everyone!' he shouted, when he felt the time was right. 'Can I have you all in the living room please,' he requested. Hugh and Ben walked into the living room. Molly threw another bundle of clothes onto the floor and then walked past Ally without saying another word. Ally's gaze drifted around the room. The sight of loss looked all too familiar.

Ally was the last to join them in the living room and she squeezed herself onto the sofa. 'Molly,' said Ben gently. 'Would you explain what this is?' he said as he slid the book towards her. Molly ran her fingers across the cover and opened it up. 'Well,' she began, tentatively. 'When Nana O died, we created this book of memories. It's got all of her sayings and pictures in it,' she explained to Ben. Ben lifted up a photograph of Molly. She glanced down and her eyes scanned across it. It was a photo they had taken on the last day at the ranch, when her parents were alive. She was outside the ranch house with Ben, Ally and Hugh. 'How about we add this to it?' asked Ben. He opened the book and turned to a blank page. Molly took a deep breath, got up and went to get some glue and a pen from a drawer.

Molly slid back into her place next to Ben, on the sofa. She bravely stuck the photograph onto the page. 'What should I write?' she whispered. There was a moment of silence before the pen began to move across the page. *To be strong is to be adaptable. It is to flow with change and all that it brings. It is knowing that it always turns out for the best, and trusting that if it doesn't, then you just change again*, she wrote.

She put the pen down, and then headed back upstairs. 'Mom,' directed Hugh at Ally. 'I think it is time for a cup of tea,' he said as Molly's words filtered through.
'I agree,' Ally said, a little startled by what Molly had just written.
Ben got up. 'I'll do some of the running around for a while,' he said. He placed his hand lovingly on Hugh's body which was slumped forwards in a tired heap.

As Ally stirred the tea, she heard a knock on the

door. When she opened it, she was greeted by a young woman. 'Hi,' said the visitor. 'I am Joy, the attorney,' the young woman explained enthusiastically. She thrust her hand out in front of her. Ally reached out and shook it.

'Please do come in,' Ally invited. 'The kettle has just boiled.' Ally stepped aside as the young woman entered the house. 'It's this way,' Ally said, as she walked back into the kitchen. She pulled out a chair at the kitchen table and sat down. She gestured for Joy to do the same. Hugh appeared and brought across Ally's tea.

'Would you like one, Miss?' he asked politely.

'Oh no, thank you,' replied Joy warmly. 'I haven't long had one.'

Ben and Molly then appeared in the kitchen doorway. Hugh brought the rest of the teas to the table and they all sat down. Joy reached down and took out an important looking black file from her bag. She glanced around at them all. 'It is for us all to hear,' Ally explained with conviction when she saw the discomfort in Joy's expression. At these words, Joy visibly relaxed.

'Firstly,' Joy began. 'I am so sorry to hear about your loss.'

'You can't lose love,' Molly piped up. 'It can only transform,' she added. Ben reached across, took Molly's hand and gave it a squeeze. 'What?' Molly said, looking confused.

Joy shuffled a few pages. 'Well,' she uttered. 'I am here to read your parent's wills. There are only a couple of things really to tell you about, and I will need to get some signatures too,' she continued. 'Firstly, Ally, you are the godmother to Molly, so under the circumstances...' Joy stated. She paused before going on. '...you have sole custody of Molly,' she concluded. Ally nodded her acknowledgment. 'Financially, it is you who will receive the payment from their life assets.'

Ally interrupted. 'I know all this,' she said gravely. 'This isn't my first time around.'

Joy stopped for a moment, a little stunned by Ally's words. 'Oh,' she replied, at a loss about what to say.

'I have set up an account in Molly's name for all money to be transferred into,' Ally continued, slightly bemused. Before Joy could even respond, Ally was already sliding over a piece of paper with all the details on it.

Joy took the paper. 'Thank you,' she said quietly. 'With regards to funeral arrangements, they have already paid for their ashes to be scattered in the forest and for two oak trees to be planted.' Molly looked across at Ally who nodded her acknowledgement.

'Apart from that, the house is to be left to Molly,'
Joy stated.

'I want to sell it,' responded Molly and she sat up
tall in her seat. Joy looked across at her, slightly
shocked by her decisiveness.

'Very well,' she replied. 'Oh yes,' Joy continued.
'There is one more thing.' She slid an envelope
out from behind the pages. 'It is addressed to you
Molly,' she said as she handed it over.

Molly reached across and took the envelope. She
surveyed the writing on it. 'This is Nana O's
handwriting,' she said as she quickly turned it
over and opened it up. A small piece of card fell
out.

'The owl is the guardian of a secret,' Molly read
aloud.

Hugh leant across. 'What does that mean?' he
asked with a puzzled frown.

'I am not too sure yet,' Molly said as she ran her
fingers across the letters.

Joy interrupted and looked at Ally. 'If I could just
have your signature here and here,' she
requested as she pointed to two boxes on a piece
of paper. 'And, I'll be in touch if there is anything
else.' Joy stood back up and Ally's signature
squiggled across the page. Joy closed the file with
a thump. 'Well, that's all,' she concluded. 'Enjoy
the rest of the day. I'll let myself out.'

Ally watched Joy walk down the corridor and reach for the handle of the front door. Just at that moment, it flung open. It was Jane returning back. She and Joy stood in front of each other, both a little startled. 'Hi,' Jane managed to stutter.

'Bye,' Joy replied as she stepped by. Jane walked inside towards the kitchen.

'That was quick,' Jane said as she headed straight for the kettle. Ally simply raised her eyebrows in response.

Molly stood up. 'There is no time for tea, Jane,' she said. 'There is another load to be taken to the charity shop before the estate agent arrives,' she ordered.

Jane stopped with the kettle suspended in mid-air, but placed it back down. 'Aye-aye, Captain,' she answered with a wink and a mock salute.

Molly held onto the note from Nana O. She twisted and turned it in her hands. The words twirled around in her mind. *The owl is the guardian of a secret*, she muttered repeatedly under her breath. But, she soon snapped out of her daze. 'Right!' she said decisively. 'Let's finish off this house.' She stood up, marched into the living room and grabbed another box. Ben, Ally and Hugh all glanced at each other.

Hugh couldn't hide his excitement any longer. 'Ooh, this is just starting to get good,' he said, rubbing his hands together. 'I love a good puzzle!' Ben and Ally chuckled. 'Ever the optimist, Monkey,' Ally said affectionately.

'Right, Hugh,' said Ben. 'Let's bring down the last of the boxes from upstairs, and we'll start on the kitchen whilst Ally and Molly pack up the living room.'

Ally stepped cautiously into the living room. 'Molly,' she said tentatively. 'Stop a moment, and come and sit down.' Molly popped her head out of the cupboard with a look of confusion. But, she walked over and plonked herself down by Ally's side. 'Are you sure you're alright?' Ally inquired. Molly stared straight into Ally's eyes. Ally watched her gaze. It was so steady and sure, and held a strength inside that could move mountains. 'Yes, I am,' Molly confirmed. 'I just wish they could have been a bit more organised, like Nana O was. She had sorted all her stuff out. Why couldn't they have done the same?' Molly questioned. She threw her arms up in the air in frustration.

Ally wrapped her arm around Molly and gave her a squeeze. 'Because some of us are a bit younger on this journey compared to your Nana,' Ally explained wisely.

Molly hugged her. 'Everything is going to be alright,' she asserted confidently.

'Aren't I meant to be the one saying that to you?' Ally questioned in jest. 'Right,' she continued. 'What shall we do with all this furniture?' she said as she glanced around the room.

Molly paused a moment and pondered Ally's question. 'Pay it forward,' she said simply. 'Ben! Hugh! Come here quick,' Molly suddenly screeched.

Ben shot through the door in a panic. 'What's wrong? What's happened?' he asked with breathless concern.

Molly began to chuckle. 'Please could you put all the furniture out on the front lawn,' she requested with a shake of her head. Ben gave Molly a sideways glance and wiggled his finger.

'We will pay it forward so someone else can build their home too,' Molly clarified. She got up and took a piece of paper out of the printer. She wrote the words, *FREE TO A GOOD HOME* on it, and placed it on the coffee table. Piece by piece, the furniture was placed outside the house. And car by car, people started to take it all away. Molly stepped back into the house which was now just an empty shell, apart from 3 boxes by the front door. Jane appeared and stood by Molly's side.

'Shall I put these in the boot of the car for you?' she asked softly. Molly just nodded silently in response.

Molly began to replay all the memories she had made in the house. With each memory, another tear fell, as she began the painful process of letting go of what was. A deep emptiness began to appear. It was like her roots had been uplifted but had no place to yet call home. Ben secretly watched Molly from behind as she lowered her barriers, for just a moment. What he saw was a little girl, full of fear. He walked up to her and placed a hand on each of Molly's shoulders. 'We will post those boxes back to the ranch,' he said reassuringly. 'So they'll be there when you get back home,' he added lovingly.

'That's it!' Molly suddenly declared. She spun around and looked at Ben. He just stared back in bewilderment. 'I have got a home,' she cried. 'I have got a family! I haven't lost anything. It has just transformed. We need to go to Nana O's house right now!' she exclaimed.
'What about the estate agent?' Ben asked.
'Ally and Hugh can sort that out,' Molly said as she grabbed Ben's hand and pulled him out the front door.

'Jane, we need you to take us to Nana O's,'

instructed Molly as she climbed purposefully into the back of the car.

Ally looked across at Ben 'What for?' she questioned.

'Apparently you and Hugh are to stay here to sort things out,' explained Ben. 'And Molly said she wants to go to Nana O's place,' he added with a shrug, before climbing into the front seat. Jane started up the engine and the car rolled off the drive.

The familiar road twisted and turned, and Molly felt her body tighten with anticipation. Nana O's cottage finally came into view and Jane slowed the car as she approached it. Molly held her breath. She nearly didn't recognise it. She saw a young woman out in the garden. The cottage looked different. It had been painted and new windows had been fitted. Even the shed was standing up straight. Molly unclipped her seat belt, opened the door and stepped out into the fresh, country air.

Ben reached over but he felt Jane's hand on his arm. 'Best leave her to it,' she whispered. Molly began to walk up the path, past the place where the photo had been taken with her parents. The young women turned around at the sound of the approaching footsteps. 'Hi,' she greeted as she stood and dusted her muddy hands on her

trousers. 'I, umm, well the thing is,' Molly stuttered. She paused and took in a steadying breath. 'My nana used to live here,' she explained. 'And she has left me something.'
'Oh, right,' said the young woman. 'Do you know where she left it?' she asked with a graceful smile.

'Well, see, that's the problem,' said Molly a little awkwardly. 'I am not too sure.' She sunk her hands into her pockets and swayed from side to side.
'Well, now,' said the woman. 'That does make it more interesting.' The woman glanced across at the car. 'Why don't I put the kettle on,' she offered kindly. 'Do your friends want to come in too?' she asked.
Molly glanced behind her. 'If it's OK, I will pass on the tea, thank you. I just need to see if the statue of the owl is still near the shed,' Molly asked carefully.
'Of course,' said the woman. 'I am sure you know the way. If you need any help, let me know. Otherwise I'll get back to planting these new seeds.' At that, the young women knelt back down. She gently picked up each individual seed and placed it lovingly in the ground.

Molly smiled gratefully and turned on her heels.

As she walked across to the shed, her adrenaline grew inside her stomach. It felt like it was filled with thousands of butterflies. She made her way around the back of the shed and spotted the statue of the owl she had been looking for. It was sitting on a branch. She quickly began to search around it, but found nothing obvious. So, she pushed it with all her might and lowered it to the ground to see if there might be anything underneath it. But, found nothing. She sat on top of the statue and placed her head in her hands. The fear she had been so carefully pushing down washed over her like a tidal wave.

'This doesn't make any sense,' she said to herself. 'Why would Nana O send me back here? I can't think of another owl or anywhere else that one would be,' she pondered. Her questions were endless as she grasped for even the smallest string of hope. But, she soon lost her fight. She slid her hands over her eyes and she wept. She felt her tears drip through her finger tips. 'Oh, Nana O,' she pleaded. 'Please help me.' A sudden gust of wind whipped up and swirled around her. It took Molly by surprise and she shivered. She peeled her hands from her cheeks, and as her eyes adjusted to the light, she saw a white feather at her feet. Molly reached down and picked it up. The strands of the feather danced tantalisingly in the breeze.

'That's odd,' murmured Molly as she wiped her tear-stained cheeks with her sleeve. She stood up and made her way back to the car. She held the feather gently between her finger tips.

'Did you find what you were looking for?' asked the young woman as she shaded her eyes from the sun with her hand.

'I am not sure,' answered Molly with a bewildered sigh. 'If this is it,' she said, holding the feather up for the woman to see. 'It's one bad joke. My Nana O said *the owl is the guardian of a secret*, so I looked by the owl and found nothing except this feather.'

The young woman shrugged and went back to tending her garden. 'There is no greater treasure than hope, belief and desire, and knowing that some things will come to be,' she said with a magical glint in her eyes. 'Stop trying to see what you expected to see and allow life to show you what it could be. Sometimes, we expect so little of ourselves, but life knows our truth and our greatest potential. Every once in a while, it reminds us to let go of the results we think we should receive, and allow life to bring what it thinks they should be. Which is normally a lot greater and better than what our imaginations can create,' she concluded knowingly.

Molly allowed the words to flow over her, but the

fear that was rapidly turning into frustration still bubbled inside. 'Well, have a lovely day,' Molly said politely before making her way back to the car.

She climbed inside and Jane turned to her. 'Any luck?' she asked.

'I don't need luck,' answered Molly. 'I have hope,' she said as she curled her fingers around the feather and stared out the window. Jane waved to the young lady who beamed a beautiful smile in response. She reversed back down the lane and Molly watched the hedgerow pass by and a familiar, single tree come into view.

Molly suddenly slammed her hands on the back of the head rest. 'Stop!' she shouted. Jane pressed her foot hard on the brake and everybody lurched forwards in their seats. Molly flung her door open and ran to the tree. She was quickly followed by Jane and Ben. They watched as Molly collapsed to her knees at the base of the tree. She started to yank and pull at the grass. She dug at the dirt frantically with her nails. Ben and Jane crouched down to try and see what Molly was doing. 'Oww!' Molly cried. She pulled her hand away and shook her throbbing fingers. 'What is it?' Ben asked as he dusted off the dirt. 'I don't know,' Molly said. 'But it is solid, that's for sure,' she added as she squeezed her sore fingers to dull the pain.

Ben carefully dug around the object, and soon noticed that it was a tin box. He pulled it out of the earth and brushed off the remaining dirt. There was an engraving of an owl on the lid. He passed it over to Molly who slowly lifted open the lid. There inside lay a feather and two folded pieces of paper. Molly carefully lifted out the first piece. She gently unfolded it and saw Nana O's handwriting. *Let the feathers bring you faith.* Molly paused to take in this treasured moment. She felt closer and closer to Nana O. She then lifted out the next piece of paper and unfolded that one too. There in her hands lay a cheque. The silence that followed was huge. But it was suddenly broken by Jane. 'Oh my goodness,' she squealed excitedly and her hands flew to her mouth.

Molly sat in complete shock. She stared again at the cheque. 'One million two hundred thousand pounds,' she read aloud. Her eyes scanned the words again and again, and then found Nana O's signature, so delicate and beautiful.

Molly turned to Ben. 'Is that a lot?' she asked naively.

Ben's smile grew. 'Well,' he answered. 'Put it this way, you'll never have to worry about money in this lifetime.' Molly placed the pieces of paper and two feathers back in the box. She held it tightly to her chest as she climbed back into the car. Jane slid back into the driver's seat, still shaking her head in disbelief. Molly went back to watching the countryside roll by. She could feel a love rising up from deep inside as her fingers squeezed around the tin box. *With just a little faith*, she thought, *life can change for the better in a single moment.*

3 THE SETTING SUN

Jane soon pulled the car back into the driveway
of Molly's house. Their attention was drawn to a
man in a blue suit who was stepping out of the
front door and shaking Ally's hand. 'Have a great
day,' he chimed as he made his way to his car.
Molly placed the box by her side and leant over
the back seat. She began to dig around in her
cardboard box. She suddenly pulled out a
beautiful blue dress, with subtle stripes down it.
Ben and Jane were already making their way
across to the house. Ben began to explain to Ally
all that had happened at Nana O's house. Molly
watched as Ally's eyes grew wide with surprise.
She took a deep breath. 'My faith is stronger than
my fears,' she whispered to herself as she
pushed the sadness down that had been trying to
creep out all day.

Molly stepped out of the car and boldly walked across to where they were standing. 'How did it go?' she asked pragmatically.

'Umm, yes. All sorted,' stuttered Ally. 'They are going to put it on the market and send any paperwork that needs filling out to my house. It should be finalised in a couple of months,' she explained.

Molly sighed with disappointment. 'So long?' she muttered.

Ally placed her hand on Molly's back. 'These things take time, lovely,' she reassured.

Molly crinkled her nose at her. 'Why should they? Why can't it be all sorted today?' she asked with an irritated sigh. She felt herself begin to get frustrated by everyone's desire for change to be so slow. 'Some of us don't mind change occurring at the speed of light!' Molly snapped. But she quickly stopped herself. 'Sorry. I didn't mean to get cross,' she said apologetically.

Ally chuckled. 'I think it's OK for you to feel whatever you want to feel, and wish whatever you want to wish,' she stated simply. 'I know you can pull a miracle out of the bag if you so want to.'

Molly smiled as she felt a sense of calmness begin to return. 'I just wish someone would walk up and ask to buy this house, right now. And then we could get all the paper work done today,' she said with a sigh as she made her way inside. She climbed the stairs, walked into her bedroom and closed the door. It felt so different now. It was like she was standing in a stranger's house. She was just getting changed into her blue dress when there was a knock at the door. 'Come in,' Molly instructed.

Ally pushed open the door. 'Wow!' she exclaimed. 'Molly, you look so beautiful,' she said admiringly. 'You're just missing one thing though.' She stepped into Molly's room, placed her handbag on the floor and began to rummage through it. She pulled out her hairbrush and a sparkly clip.

Molly stood a little taller as Ally brushed her hair and secured the clip in place. 'There,' said Ally. 'Perfection. I was actually just coming to tell you that we are ready to head off, if you are,' she said, giving Molly a well-needed squeeze.

Molly spun around on her heels. She felt like a diamond. Like something precious and beautiful that had been created from immense pressure. 'Totally ready!' Molly responded with a smile. They both made their way down to the front door and Ally handed the key to Molly.

'I'll meet you in the car,' said Ally. Molly glanced across and saw that Jane, Ben and Hugh were already waiting.

Molly felt the familiar punch of fear in her stomach. She slid the key into the lock and heard it click. 'Excuse me,' said a voice behind her. Molly's feelings whipped back into their hiding place as she glanced over her shoulder to find a lady standing there. She didn't recognise her. 'Are your mum and dad at home, by any chance?' asked the lady.

Molly paused. She wasn't sure what she was meant to say. 'Umm...no,' she muttered. 'They have died.'

'Oh!' cried the lady, who stopped in her tracks. She clearly had no idea if she should continue or not.

Molly watched the lady shuffle uncomfortably, and drop her eye contact. *I guess I'll have to get used to this reaction*, she thought. Molly turned, stepped towards the lady and smiled. 'I am just sorting everything out before the house goes up for sale,' she explained.

'Hmm, what a coincidence,' replied the lady with a curious frown. 'That's kind of what I was coming to talk about. I suppose it's you I now need to talk to.'

'Do you want to buy it?' Molly asked confidently. Her directness took the lady a little by surprise. 'Well, yes,' she answered. 'Actually, I do.'

Molly clapped her hands together. 'Well,' she said with a smile. 'There is no time like the present to get a job done. If you like, we can head to the estate agents now and get the paperwork all signed.'

'Yes,' replied the lady. 'I would like that very much. You're very confident for a little girl. How old are you?' asked the lady, still trying to process the events unfolding before her.
'I may be young,' answered Molly. 'But I have lived a lot of life already. More than most,' she added with a twinkle. 'If you would like to follow us, we can head off now.'
The lady glanced across at the car and saw that they were being eagerly watched. 'Yes, that would be great,' she stammered before walking back to her car and climbing in.

Molly paused a moment and did a little dance. She swung her body from side to side and flapped her arms. But quickly stopped when it dawned on her that Ally, Ben, Jane and Hugh were all watching her and failing miserably to hide their giggles. Molly marched over to the car, opened the door and got in. 'I might get someone to open doors for me, you know,' Molly said arrogantly.

Ben turned to look at her. 'Multimillionaire or not, you'll still have to do chores and shovel poo at the ranch,' he said, adding a harsh pinch of reality to the moment.

Molly chuckled as she looked at Ally. Ally focused and tried to decipher what had just happened.
'Where to next?' she asked slowly.
'The estate agents please,' answered Molly with a grin.
Jane spun around in her seat to look at Molly. 'No way!' she exclaimed.
Ally began to laugh as she tapped a number into her phone.
Jane glanced across at Ally. 'How does she...? I mean...? This isn't possible! It's just...,' stuttered Jane in disbelief.
'Hello,' said Ally into the phone, interrupting Jane's blabbering. 'Hi, it's Ally,' she continued. 'I was just ringing ahead to say you'll need to be printing off that paperwork. We will be bringing along a buyer in around 20 minutes. Yes, that's correct. No chain, ready to sign. Like I said, we'll be there in 20 minutes. Yes, again, that's correct. A buyer. Bye.' Ally turned to Jane. 'I don't think you're the only one who is shocked,' she chuckled.

Molly sat, lost in thought as she took in her last memory that she would ever make at this house. 'You can either react or respond to life,' she whispered. 'If you respond, opportunities will be knocking at your door,' she added quietly. Ben silently smiled to himself as they made their way, once more, down the road.

Ben, Hugh and Jane sat patiently in the car as they watched the estate agent buzz around and pull out pieces of paper from every direction. Molly, Ally and the lady were an interesting spectacle. Hugh started to tap his fingers on his knees. A plan began to formulate with the beat he found, as his thoughts followed the rhythm.

'Ben?' Hugh said distantly.

'Yes, Son,' answered Ben, his gaze still fixed on Molly and Ally.

'It has been a bit of a tough time, hasn't it?' Hugh said, a little more focused now.

'Yep,' confirmed Ben. 'Not had a day this tough, not since...' Ben stopped himself and turned to look at Hugh. 'Why do you ask?' he queried.

'Well, I have been thinking,' Hugh began.

'Oh no!' said Jane, rolling her eyes. 'Here we go!'

'No, it's a good kind of thinking,' explained Hugh. 'I am watching Molly unthread the tapestry of her old life, and I just think that maybe we should go away. You know, to just recharge her,' Hugh suggested as he scanned the row of shops.

'Oh, don't worry,' interjected Jane confidently. 'Molly is fine. She's taking it all in her stride,' she concluded confidently.

Ben's eyebrows became scrunched. 'I wouldn't be so sure about that,' he said with concern. 'The dam can only hold the flood back for so long before the cracks begin to grow. It's not a case of if the dam will burst, but when.'

Jane and Ben looked at each other, a little worried, as Hugh unclipped his seat belt and jumped out of the car. Ben watched as Hugh crossed the road to a bookstore, disappear behind a stand of books and then reappear by the check out. Hugh then walked briskly back to the car, swinging a carrier bag in his right hand. He climbed in without saying a single word.

'*Ting-ting*' went Ben's phone. It was a text from Ally: *All done! Can you believe it? A xx*. Ben looked back into the estate agents to see Ally and Molly standing up and shaking the agent's hand. He watched as they made their way out to the car. This time, the exhaustion could no longer be hidden by Molly. She gently closed her eyes as she was engulfed by tiredness.

A short while later, Molly awoke and looked sleepily around the car. She spotted Ally's front door. It was dusk outside and she could see a welcome light shining out from the living room. She climbed wearily out of the car, but stopped for a moment. As her feet touched the pavement, her legs began to buckle beneath her. Molly took a deep breath in and waddled to the front door. She pushed it open and stepped inside. She was greeted by the sight of Ally and Ben on the sofa, and Jane in the chair with a cup of tea. Ally stood up immediately. 'Are you ready for your dinner?' she asked gently, guiding an unsteady Molly to another chair.

'No. I am good, thank you,' answered Molly. 'I think I am going to go and have a shower and wash the day off.' As she attempted to stand back up, her legs now felt like lead. What was happening?

Before she knew it, Ben had scooped her onto his back and was carrying her upstairs. Ally followed. 'Maybe a bath might be better,' Ally said. She headed to the bathroom and began to run a nice hot bath while Molly got undressed. Ben silently made his way across to Hugh's bedroom door. He peered through the tiny crack and saw Hugh on his bed, surrounded by magazines and an open map. Ben slowly opened the door, trying not to let it creak, but to no avail. Hugh sat with his arms across his chest and stared straight at Ben. 'Are you sneaking up on me?' he asked jokily.

'Me?' answered Ben with mock surprise. 'Of course not,' he added playfully, wafting his hand dismissively in front of him.

Ben looked across at the wall. 'So, this is the original Diary of Dreams?' he asked with open admiration.

Hugh leapt to his feet and jumped onto his bed. 'Yep! This is where it all began,' replied Hugh. 'Yet now, when I look at it, it seems like such a small, achievable dream. But, when I first made it, I thought none of this would ever happen,' Hugh said, shaking his head. 'You can be, do and have anything you want,' responded Ben wisely. 'As long as you are prepared to take the journey and its tests,' he said to himself as he remembered the words of his grandpa.

Hugh plonked himself down onto the bed. 'What do you mean?' he asked with a puzzled look. Ben took in a deep breath. 'Many of us have dreams,' he began. 'Yet the majority of people lose the courage needed to follow them. And this can happen before they have even started. It's not because they don't want them. Because, if anything, they want them so bad. It's because of the test that the journey holds for them,' Ben said as he lowered himself down next to Hugh.

'The tests aren't there to prevent us from succeeding,' Ben continued. 'They are there to teach us, and to make things uncomfortable so that we change, inside and out. But because of how people choose to look at these tests, they normally stop trying after the first attempt, because it seems difficult. Yet, it's actually all just relative.'

'What do you mean by *relative*?' Hugh asked, scrunching up his nose.

'Most things in life are neutral,' Ben explained. 'It is us who decides what is good or bad, hard or easy, achievable or not, something to worry about or enjoy. These judgements have been taught to us when we are very small, so that we, hopefully, turn out to be good people. But, where it goes wrong, is actually when we make the wrong judgement - when we begin to compare our dreams to others, or everything around us.'

'Hang on,' said Hugh, a little overwhelmed. 'Let me get this right. It's not the actual thing that's the problem. It's what we compare it to which makes it seem good or bad?' he questioned, his eyes alight with intensity.

'Yes,' answered Ben simply. 'If you compare a situation or one of your dreams to climbing Mount Everest, then of course it will seem tough. Maybe even an unachievable dream. But, if you compared that same situation to, say, you and your mum getting on a plane, then you would probably feel that you could succeed. It's not what you dream or how big you dream. It's what you compare that dream to that makes it achievable or unachievable.'

Hugh's gaze drifted down to the map that lay on the floor. 'What about the tests?' he asked. 'Do we always have the tests?'
Ben smiled gently. 'Always,' he confirmed. 'That's a guarantee. Most of us don't find it easy to let go or change, so life helps us out by making things uncomfortable. This then forces us to move past our fear and have faith that we can get through the change, to find comfort once more, but maybe in a different place.'

Hugh rested his chin on his hands as he looked up at his dream wall. 'Yes,' he pondered. 'There were many opportunities to give up when we met you. Many times that we had to do things, even though they were scary. But it was always worth it,' Hugh muttered.
Ben leant back and let his head rest against the wall. 'Well, each test depends on which season of your dream you are in,' he stated. 'Each season has a different purpose.'
Hugh laid back and swung his legs across Ben's. 'Now you have definitely lost me!' he exclaimed with a shake of his head.
Ben smiled wisely. 'Think of it like this,' he said. 'Winter is a time to re-evaluate and check that

everything is going in the right direction. Spring is a time to add something new to the dream or make it bigger. Summer is all about protecting your ideas and dreams from those who may want to prevent them coming true. And Autumn is a time to receive or bring a dream to completion.'

Hugh became lost in thought as his toes wiggled with excitement. 'So,' inquired Ben. 'Are you going to let me in on your plan?' he asked as he gestured to the map on the floor with his eyes. 'What plan?' asked Hugh cheekily. 'I don't have a plan!'
Ben burst out into laughter. 'Hugh, you always have a dream on the go, and a plan to go with it for that matter!' he stated as his laughter began to subside.
Hugh rolled off the bed. 'Well, seeing as you asked,' he responded as he held up a map of the United Kingdom.
Ben leant forward to get a closer look. He saw arrows and notes by the side. 'Is this another road trip?' he asked.

'I guess I just think there are some magical places I would like to see before we go back to the ranch,' explained Hugh. 'And I think it would be good for Molly too,' he added.
The bedroom door suddenly creaked again. This

time, Ally's head appeared around the frame. Her eyes shot immediately across to Hugh, who was still holding the map. 'Oh no you don't,' she said sternly, instantly regretting what she had said at the airport. 'We have enough on our plate without one of your dream maps,' she stated. 'Absolutely out of the question. Forget I ever asked.' Ally's hard look shot from Hugh to Ben in order to put a full stop on anymore planning.

Just then, a sleepy Molly appeared by Ally's side, rubbing her eyes. 'What dream map?' she asked casually.
'Nothing, love' said Ally. 'Let's get you to bed,' she said, steering Molly back out the door. She glanced back over her shoulder at Hugh and Ben, to make sure they both understood her message.

Hugh watched them leave and then promptly picked up his pen. He continued to add the finishing touches to the map. 'What Mom really meant was, *let's talk about it in the morning,*' Hugh said with a cheeky smile as he folded the map back up.
Ben grinned as he lifted himself off the bed. 'You know her best,' he said. 'But I do think it is time for bed. It has been a long day for all of us.' He made his way out of the door as Hugh took his pyjamas into the bathroom.

Ben slowly made his way down the stairs. Each step revealed the weight of the day and the heaviness he was feeling. He heard Jane clearing away in the kitchen. 'Right,' she said. 'I am heading off. I'm ready for a hot bath myself.'
'Thank you for all your help today, Jane,' Ben said, giving her a hug.
'Well, I think we should all take note of how Molly has been today,' said Jane. 'And practice some of her tricks ourselves,' she added with a smile, before making her way to the front door.

Ben leant heavily against the kitchen worktop. As he scanned the kitchen, he tried to glimpse into Ally's past. He was still trying to add little bits of detail to the parts of her story that were yet untold. Ally suddenly appeared in the kitchen doorway, snapping Ben out of his thoughts. He smiled wearily. 'We made it through the day,' he said with an exhausted but accomplished sigh. Ally moved across and wrapped her arms around Ben's waist. She rested her head on his chest and their breathing became synchronised, almost automatically. She let her eyes close and she listened intently to his heartbeat. She felt his fingers gently run down her back as he held onto her, tightly. He knew it wasn't just Molly who was grieving.

Ally slowly opened her eyes and her lids flickered as they adjusted to the bright kitchen light. She pulled herself away from Ben. 'I am heading up to bed,' she said. Ben held onto to her hand as she began to walk away. But he gently pulled her back into his arms for a kiss. Ally felt her body tingle with love and joy. She could not supress the smile that beamed involuntarily across her face as she made her way towards the stairs. Ben watched Ally walk away and his fingers began to tap lightly on his jeans. His thoughts began to gather momentum and his fingers suddenly stopped in mid-air. A thought suddenly flashed through his mind and a smile crept across his face. He pushed off from the worktop, switched off the light and climbed the stairs. He was surprised to discover that he was humming as he went.

The morning sunlight was a mixture of golds and reds, and it shone through Hugh's bedroom window. He sneaked silently out of bed, took his map from under his pillow and crept downstairs. He was afraid that Ally might have taken it whilst he slept. He spread it out on the living room floor and became captivated as he made a few adjustments to his plan. Hugh heard the distant sound of a key turning in the lock of the front door. He glanced up as it swung open and a whirl wind swept in, along with his grandma. 'Hi,

Grandma,' he said distractedly before quickly turning back to his map. His grandma disappeared through the kitchen and up the stairs. Hugh's eyes suddenly enlarged as the realisation dawned on him. 'Grandma!' he shrieked and bolted towards the stairs, but he was already too late.

Ally's mum waltzed brazenly into Ally's bedroom, marched straight over to the window and ripped back the curtains. Her usual, whirlwind style instantly whipped up a stormy atmosphere. 'And when were you going to tell me you were back?' she asked with an accusatory tone. She placed her hands on her hips and focused on the picture before her. Shock quickly descended. 'Grandma! Grandma, wait, don't go into Mum's room,' cried Hugh breathlessly as he ran up the stairs. But, again, he was too late. Ben slowly rolled over and coughed to try and clear his thoughts. 'Mam,' he said, nodding his head in acknowledgment. He tried to hide the fact that he was frantically nudging Ally with his elbow under the duvet.

'What?' asked Ally croakily as she yawned and stretched. But she suddenly sat bolt upright in bed at the sight of their guest. 'Mum,' she said slowly. Ally's mum stood in the morning light. Her face was illuminated by the glow and it moulded

into many expressions. Her jaw moved up and down, yet no words could find their way out.
'I think I will go and put the kettle on,' she muttered awkwardly. But she continued to stare intensely at Ben. She moved robotically around the bed, and Hugh, who was bent over trying to catch his breath.
'Sorry Mom, I tried to warn her,' Hugh gasped. Ally flopped back down and stuffed a pillow over her head. She let out a low groan.

Ben and Hugh began to chuckle and Ally felt the bed shake. 'It's not funny!' she said in a muffled pillow-voice. But this caused Ben and Hugh to descend into an even bigger, belly-roaring laugh. Ally playfully threw the pillow at Ben who caught it with no effort. 'Well, I best go and deal with it now rather than putting it off,' Ally said grudgingly. She lifted her body into an upright position before putting on her dressing gown and disappearing out of the bedroom.

Hugh climbed onto the bed and sat next to Ben. They listened eagerly to Ally's footsteps tread down the stairs and then the slamming of a cupboard door in the kitchen. Ally's and her mum's words flew across the kitchen, like a tennis match. Ben let out another little chuckle. 'So, that's THE grandma?' he asked as he folded his arms across his chest.

'Just you wait,' said Hugh.

'I don't permit a stranger in my daughter's bed!' Ally's mum shouted near the bottom of the stairs. She clearly wanted the whole house to hear her opinion.

'He's not a stranger, Mum,' explained Ally. 'He is my fiancé,' she retorted.

There was a deathly moment of silence and then a shriek. 'Fiance?' Ally's mum yelled.

Ben looked at Hugh and raised his eyebrows. 'I don't suppose you have any tin hats at the bottom of your wardrobe, do you?' he asked with a chuckle.

Hugh smiled. 'Ben, can I ask you a question?' he said tentatively.

'Always, Champion,' Ben replied altering his position so that he was facing Hugh.

'Well, you know what you were saying last night? That a problem is only as big as what you compare it to? Well, do you think that yesterday was Molly's life-test to remember something?' Hugh queried.

Ben ran his fingers through his hair and pondered the thought. 'I believe Molly has learnt some things about herself that maybe she didn't quite believe were true,' he offered. 'For instance, how wise and confident she is, and most of all, how adaptable. Those skills will set her in good stead in life. Some people may get completely derailed from events like the ones Molly went through. But, Molly decided to keep everything in perspective. And, most importantly, she never lost her faith in herself that she would be able to cope and be OK. That is invaluable,' he concluded.

Hugh shuffled down the bed so that he was laying down, looking up at the ceiling. 'I wonder what my test will be,' he asked rhetorically.

Ben patted him before climbing out of bed and getting dressed. 'I best go and rescue your mum,' he said. 'It's gone a bit too quiet down there for my liking.'

Hugh suddenly sat bolt upright. 'My map!' he cried as he thrust himself off the bed. 'I don't want Mom to see it! Not yet, anyway,' he said as he darted in front of Ben.

They both then made their way downstairs and entered the kitchen. They were greeted by an invisible wall of tension, a cobra ready to strike. Ally and her mum were sitting opposite each other at the kitchen table. They were staring, unblinking, at each other, each waiting for the other to speak first.

Hugh slithered past them and entered the living room, to quickly retrieve his map. Ben gently coughed to try and break the spell that seemed to have been cast over Ally and her mum. He was also keen to override the growing feeling of fear that seemed to be stirring inside. 'Morning, Mam,' he ventured kindly. 'You must be Ally's mom? Hi, I am Ben,' he said and took an unsteady step towards the table. He held out his hand, an offer of a white flag, but he wasn't quite sure which way these two bulls were going to charge. Ally's mum didn't move. She just shifted her stern gaze to Ben and then back to Ally.

'Oh, come on, Mum!' said Ally as she rolled her eyes. 'Give it a rest. I am more than old enough now to choose a man for myself! I thought you would be pleased that I am no longer spending my mornings in a heap of tears on the kitchen floor,' she said. She pushed her chair back from the kitchen table and stood up. She moved instinctively in front of Ben, ready to be his protective shield against her mum's harsh words. Ally's mum slowly stood too and the tension intensified. Hugh cautiously made his way into the kitchen just as Ally's mum raised her hand, her finger pointing sharp, like a razor.

Hugh took a giant stride and slammed his map down, hard, on the table. 'I have had enough of this,' he yelled. 'One of my best friends had the worst day of her life yesterday. And here you both

are, worrying about Ben! Grandma, I love Ben,
like a dad. I love seeing Mom so happy every day.
And also having Ben's help with keeping her in
line. He has opened his heart and home for me,
Mom and now Molly, with no hesitation. We all
have dreams, Grandma,' he continued. 'And
some are worth fighting for and protecting,
especially when you feel like the whole world is
against you.'

Ally's mum took a step back, the shock clearly
evident on her face. She blinked a few times and
then something seemed to shift, as if she was
being transported away from her rage. She
quickly took hold of Hugh and flung her arms
around. She squeezed him tightly. 'That is all I
ever wanted for you both,' she whispered.
'Happiness, love and a home.'
Ally shuffled uncomfortably as the realisation
descended. 'I know I should have gone about this
in a better way,' she said shakily. 'I am doing the
best I can right now though,' she explained as
she moved across to hug her mum.

'I think it's time for some more tea,' interrupted
Ben. 'To celebrate,' he added awkwardly. But, the
moment was disturbed by the sound of light
footsteps coming down the stairs. It was Molly.
Ally quickly sprang into action. 'Morning, love,'
she said with a smile. 'How did you sleep?' She

instantly regretted the question though. She could already see the answer in the dark rings under Molly's eyes. Molly smiled wearily as she walked over to Ben.

He instantly scooped her up into his arms. 'Morning, Miss Sunshine,' he greeted, holding her closely. He felt Molly melt into the hug.

Ally's mum shuffled uncomfortably at the closeness. 'I best be off,' she said with a small cough. 'I have so many jobs to do and so many people to tell your news to,' she shouted over her shoulder. And then, *whoosh*, she was out the door.

Hugh slid into a chair. His head lay heavily in his hands as he leant his elbows on the kitchen table. 'I thought we could go and visit a few places while we are here,' he said. 'You know, show Ben around,' he added, trying to lighten the mood. His idea was greeted by a sigh from Ally. But Ben looked across to Ally. 'I would love that,' he said, giving her a cheeky wink.

Hugh's head shot up. 'Really?' he asked with wide eyes. 'You really mean it?' But before either Ally or Ben had time to respond, he whipped out the map and laid it out on the kitchen table. He ironed out the creases with the palm of his hand. Molly wriggled her way free from Ben's hug and wandered over to the table. Her feet were like heavy lumps of concrete. Hugh's eyes began to twinkle with delight. 'Look, Molly,' he said eagerly as he pointed his finger at the first post-it note on the map.

'We start here,' he began. 'At the waterfalls, and then we carry on going up that road there, and then go to that place,' he explained. Molly tentatively followed Hugh's finger as it slid gracefully up the map, and stopped at a large lake. Ally's curiosity got the better of her too and she peered over Hugh's shoulder.
'Why those places?' she asked. She was puzzled about where this seed of an idea had come from.

Hugh shuffled uncomfortably in his seat.
'Because, sometimes we need to put some effort into protecting our dreams,' he stated. 'There will be things that come along that will try and push them away. The waterfalls are like the wishes of millions of people, cascading over the rocks and then being taken by the rivers. That's where they need to go, to come true. And the large lake is in a place that is still mainly owned by Mother Nature - a place of truth. So, I kind of thought that we could make a wish at the waterfalls and then go up higher, to find a truth that will help make that wish come true.'

'I know it may sound silly,' he said. 'But those places just feel right, that's all,' he concluded. His voice began to soften as he heard his words out loud. He couldn't prevent feelings of doubt begin to rise up. Was he just being foolish?

Ben stepped across, pulled out a chair and opened his mouth to speak. But Ally jumped in. 'Look, Monkey,' she said to Hugh. 'Things don't always have to make sense, or be perfectly planned. Sometimes we just have to follow our hunches - our gut feelings. Because the truth is, life isn't logical. It's magical, which means there are so many endless possibilities and destinations. You just have to choose the path,' she concluded as she ruffled his hair. 'I best make some reservations then,' she said with a playful roll of her eyes, before disappearing back upstairs to get dressed.

Ben frowned. 'Hmmm...,' he said. 'I think I have a bit of competition for title of the wise owl in this family.' They all began to chuckle.

Molly's thoughts raced around her mind. Her brain felt scrambled as she struggled to take hold of just one of those thoughts. She felt her eyelids close as she pushed down the fresh set of tears that were trying to break free. 'I'd like to do it,' she said bravely. 'I am ready to get away from this place and never come back,' she choked as she ran into the living room and threw herself onto the sofa.

Ben raised his eyebrows at Hugh. 'OK! OK, I'm going,' Hugh responded as he slid his chair out from the table with a squeak. Hugh flopped down on the sofa and lay next to Molly. 'I kind of don't know what to say to make it better,' he muttered. Molly buried her face into the cushions even further. 'Some moments, Hugh,' she sobbed. 'Are beyond words.'
A single tear escaped out the corner of Hugh's eye as he listened to Molly's pain-soaked words.

4 WISHES IN THE WATERFALLS

As the morning passed, Hugh began to put his plan into action. 'Come on, slow coaches!' he called frantically, trying to herd everybody out of the house. 'Country road, take me home...,' he began to sing. Molly playfully dragged her feet as slowly as she could out of the front door, dragging her suitcase dramatically behind her. She felt less weighed down by her feelings. 'Oh my goodness!' cried Hugh with mock despair. 'I have aged 40 years already!' he wailed.

'Well you get in the car then,' snapped Ally, as her final string of patience broke. Hugh stuck out his tongue in response. He waddled out the front door and into the car that Jane had kindly leant to them. He was greeted there by a chuckling Molly.

Ben was next to climb in and click his seat belt

into place. 'Ready to rock n roll,' he said as he slapped both hands excitedly down on his legs. They all turned as their final member appeared – Ally. She closed the door and began to turn the key. But before the final click of the lock, she took in a deep breath. The last time she did this, her whole life transformed. 'Oh boy,' she thought. 'What on earth is in store for me this time?' she muttered. She turned to find three sets of eyes staring at her and forced a smile to hide her fears.

Ally slid into the driver's seat and closed the door. She saw a little hand thread through, between the seats, holding a feather. 'Our faith is stronger than our fears,' Molly whispered. Ally reached down and gratefully took the feather. She placed it in front of her on the dash board, and felt a welcome glimmer of hope begin to bubble up. Ally turned the key in the ignition and the car roared into life. 'Here we go again!' she sang, as they began to drive down the road.

The car was silent except for the faint noise of the radio in the background. Everyone watched the scenery begin to transform. The higher up the country they drove, fields turned into open valleys, and straight roads transformed into twisted lanes. They no longer cut through the land, but rolled with the hills. Molly's and Hugh's eyes were fixed on the ever-changing view out of the car window as the minutes turned into hours.

Molly's mind flashed back to the country road she used to travel down to see Nana O. A tear glistened on her cheek, but she quickly brushed it away. 'Have you made a wish in the waterfall before, Hugh?' asked Molly.
'Nope,' he answered. 'But, I have my wish ready.' Hugh reached into his pocket and took out a tiny piece of paper. He smiled shyly at Molly before quickly stuffing it back in, where no one could see it.

Ben turned around in his seat. 'Do you know your wish, Molly?' he asked. Molly reached in and took hold of the locket that still hung protectively around her neck. She nodded but said nothing more. Ben looked across to Ally. She was busy muttering to herself as her grip got progressively tighter around the steering wheel. He placed his hand reassuringly on her lap. 'Is everything OK?' he asked thoughtfully.
'Why?' Ally questioned with an exasperated sigh. 'Why does she have to get involved? She's already organising me and bossing me around. Does she not think I can blood...' Ally stopped herself going any further as she glanced Hugh's and Molly's expression in the rear-view mirror. 'Flippin' organise something for myself. I told you

not to tell her! I told you it was a bad idea,' she continued. 'But, oh no! No one listens to me.' Her face reddened with rage.

'Mom,' interrupted Hugh. 'Breathe, before you start to turn purple,' he instructed quickly. Ally took a huge gulp of air and her shoulders slumped heavily.

Ben couldn't stop the smile that was growing from deep inside and turning into a wide grin. Ally turned the car sharply to the left, knocking him off balance. 'After all that I have just said,' she cried. 'You are sitting there, grinning like the cat who got the cream.'

Ben's smile grew even wider. Deep inside, he knew the secret. Hugh then started to chuckle, quickly followed by Molly. Molly reached forward and tapped Ally gently on the shoulder. 'It'll be alright,' she managed to splutter through her laughter.

Ally's expression turned into one of confusion. 'What is it that you lot know that I don't?' she inquired. Ben quickly turned his head to look out of the window, hoping to hide his expression. Ally had had enough. She swerved the car into a layby and yanked on the hand brake. 'Right, you troublesome bunch,' she said determinedly. 'Time to talk. And you best get on with it pretty quickly, otherwise I am getting out of this car and you can drive yourselves there!'

That was the tipping point. Everyone in the car suddenly erupted with laughter. Nobody was able to hold it inside any longer. They had reached the end of their surprise. Ally reached for the car door handle, but Ben instantly signalled for her to wait. He caught his breath and began to explain. 'OK, just give me a second,' he said as he regained control of his giggles.

'Ally,' he began. 'I think you know by now that I am a gentleman. You didn't honestly think I would ask for the honour of spending the rest of my life with you without asking your mom first, did you?' he questioned.
Ally's expression seemed to run through a whole spectrum of emotions, like endless waves across her body. She went from anger, to shock, back to anger, to surprise, and then eventually settled on disbelief. Ally turned in her seat. 'You knew about this?' she asked, looking directly at Molly and Hugh. They both proudly nodded their heads.

Ben leant forward and combed his fingers through Ally's hair. His eyes were alive with the spark of unconditional love as he leaned in to kiss her. 'I asked Hugh first, if it was OK,' he explained. 'And then I Face-timed your mom before we went to Yellow Stone. I am afraid to say that, yesterday, she was acting. And incredibly well too!' Ben paused, trying to assess how much trouble he was in.

But Ally fell silent. It was deathly quiet as she turned the ignition and pulled out of the layby. Ben shuffled uneasily. He could cope with angry, but the silence was cutting through him like a thousand knives. Ally continued to drive and they soon saw an old, stone cottage up ahead. It was tucked away on a hillside, with just a single track leading towards it.

Ally pulled up in front of the cottage. The only noise to be heard was the crunching of the gravel under the wheels. She parked the car just in front of the cottage's red door. She paused a moment and tuned into the whistling of a gentle breeze as it wound through the branches of an old oak tree. She didn't know what to say because she didn't know what she felt. Was it relief? Did she feel numb or angry? Or, did she feel invisible? She let out a small groan as the weight of the last few days suddenly hit her like a hurricane. 'We had better get settled in,' she said before stepping outside.

Ben, Molly and Hugh all looked at each other. 'Well, I wasn't expecting that,' said Hugh, dumbfounded and confused.

'I'll unpack the car,' offered Ben.

'And I'll make Ally a cup of tea,' said Molly.

'OK, I'll go and talk to Mom,' Hugh added, feeling like he had drawn the short straw.

Hugh stepped out of the car and wandered across to Ally who was sitting at the bottom of the oak tree. She had her eyes closed and her breathing had found a new, much softer rhythm. Hugh sat down next to her and snuggled up close. She instinctively wrapped her arm around him and pulled him closer. Hugh waited a second before speaking. 'Mom?' he whispered tentatively. 'Are you OK?' He felt that this moment should not be tainted with words.

Ally let out a deep sigh as she slowly opened her eyes. She blinked against the bright sunlight and then let her eyes drift over the rolling valley. The fields criss-crossed all the way to the horizon, like a large patchwork quilt, and large boulders jutted out of the hillside. Hugh felt Ally squeeze him tighter. 'I think so,' she answered eventually. 'I don't actually know. I am just starting to feel like I am having to climb fewer mountains in life and more mole hills. Both still take effort, of course, but I seem to be moving through my days a little easier now. You have a big part to play in that, you know,' she directed at Hugh with pride.

'We all have desires of the heart,' she

continued. 'But, committing to one takes courage. For most people, those desires never grow into anything bigger than a dream. They let their fear lead, instead of their faith. But when two lives are combined, each person is not just believing in themselves. They are also putting their faith in the other person's dreams and desires. And having faith in them that they too have the courage to follow their heart's desires. I have done that once before with your dad.' Ally's gaze drifted upwards to the passing clouds. 'But, to love, and then to lose that love, is a pain hope to never feel again. Yet my faith has been stronger than that fear as I now make that same commitment to Ben.' Ally couldn't help smile as his name passed through her lips, a word so sweet.

Hugh frowned. 'I think I understand,' he said, looking at Ally, still a little confused. Ally's smile grew as she reached across to tickle Hugh, and his laughter echoed through the valley.
They were interrupted by the arrival of Molly with a welcome cup of tea. 'I thought you might be ready for one,' she said as she passed it to Ally and sat down.
'Thank you, Molly,' Ally responded with genuine gratitude.
Ben came around the other side of the tree and

wrapped his arm around Ally. He kissed her on the top of her head. 'So, how much trouble am I in, you guys?' he asked, looking at Hugh and Ally. Ally glanced up and gave Ben a soft kiss on his lips. 'None at all,' she whispered.

They all sat a while longer to watch the sun dip behind the other side of the valley. They saw the sky transform from bright blue to ruby red, as the old oak tree shielded and protected them from the gentle breeze. Ben readjusted his position. 'I think we best be heading in and get set up for the night,' he suggested. Ally tried to move, but her body was so incredibly relaxed. More than she had ever felt. It was like her heart had been anchored down and prevented from moving forwards, but was now released.

Ally looked across at Hugh and Molly. Their heads were perfectly balanced together and they had both fallen asleep. Ally silently nudged Ben and pointed at the sleeping pair. Ben glanced over and smiled. 'I think we were all ready to see life from a different angle,' he said.
Ally gently rocked Hugh. He stretched and wriggled, and slowly opened his eyes. It took a while for his focus to adjust and Ally to become less blurry. 'We had best head in,' Ally suggested, nodding towards the stone cottage.

They all clambered up and began to make their way inside. As they stepped through the red front door, they were greeted by an open-plan living and kitchen area with a navy-blue sofa. The large windows were like live, framed photos of the countryside, and there was a spiral staircase leading up to the bedrooms. Hugh felt his body begin to wake up as he powered across to a box by the side of the sofa. He pulled out a board game and a pack of cards. 'Maybe we could play with one of these after dinner,' he suggested, holding them up.

'Sounds like a great idea,' confirmed Ally as she scanned the worktops for the tea bags. She felt a gentle touch on her shoulder. 'Let's go out for dinner,' whispered Ben into her ear.
Ally let her head fall back onto his chest and she closed her eyes. 'Mmm,' she agreed. 'That's a perfect idea.' Ally twirled round, wrapped her arms around him and nestled her head into his neck. For the first time, she felt their hearts beat at the same time.

'Right everyone! Grab your things and let's go and find a pub for dinner,' Ally said enthusiastically. She untangled herself from Ben and grabbed her handbag. She marched straight back out the door, with Hugh, Molly and Ben hot on her heels.

They all jumped into the car and headed back towards the road. They scanned the landscape for life, not really knowing where the road was going to take them. It eventually led them into a nearby village. 'There's one!' shouted Molly, pressing her finger against the window.

'That'll do for me,' Ally replied and she steered the car towards the pub. She pulled up outside the front, which was lined with benches. They all hopped out and Hugh took the lead as they filed inside. They were greeted by low, black beams on the ceiling, a lazy dog asleep under a table and the gentle hum of relaxed conversation.

Ally stepped forward. 'Are you still serving?' she asked the bartender politely.

'Yes, of course,' she answered. 'Take a seat and I'll be over with some menus.'

Ally nodded and followed Hugh, who was already making a bee-line for a table next to the fire. They each took their place and Molly couldn't help but watch Ben's expression. It was constantly changing as he took in the curious sight of this tiny pub.

Ally noticed Ben's quizzical look too. 'You don't get off the ranch very often, do you?' she said in jest.

'No, Mam,' Ben replied formally. 'But, I do like

what I see. It's nice to be able to create my own memories in the places you have described. It's helping me to understand you a little more,' he said as he draped his arm easily over the back of Ally's chair.

They were interrupted then by the bartender. She carefully handed out a menu to each of them.

'Can I take your drinks order first?' she asked.

'An orange juice for me,' said Hugh.

'I'll have the same, thanks,' said Ally distractedly as she scanned the menu.

'Umm, a lemonade for me,' Molly smiled.

'And for you, Sir?' asked the bartender, looking at Ben.

He blushed. 'Umm, I'll have a lemonade as well, please.'

The bartender stuffed her notepad back into her pocket. 'Just come up to the bar when you're ready to order,' she instructed.

'Actually, I can tell you now if you like?' said Ally and she reeled off each of their choices.

Hugh reached under the table and secretly slid Ally's handbag closer to him. He pulled it up onto his legs and began to rummage through. 'There it is!' he cried. He lifted a pad of post-it notes out, and a pen.

'Hey, Monkey,' exclaimed Ally as she realised her handbag was no longer where she had left it.

'Never mind that, Mom,' replied Hugh. 'Here is one for you. And one for you, and one for you,' he said as he placed a post-it note in front of each of them.

'And what are these meant to be for?' asked Molly, wafting hers in the air.

'To write your wishes on,' explained Hugh with a roll of his eyes. He thought it was pretty obvious.

'Of course! Why didn't I think of that?' Molly retorted, sarcastically. Hugh smirked at her. Molly reached across and took the pen. She carefully wrote down her wish and then slid the pen across to Ben, before folding up her post-it note.

Ben's pen hovered over his note but his mind fell blank. *What is it that I truly want*? There are so many things that society says he needs, but what is it that his heart really yearns for? He passed the pen onto Ally. 'I need a little time to think,' he said and slid the blank post-it note into his jeans pocket.

Ally paused and tried to read Ben's expression. She had never seen him hesitate before. He had always been so sure of everything. She felt fear begin to rise inside. She momentarily pushed it away and wrote down her wish.

'I shall be the keeper of your wishes,' said Hugh collecting them all up. 'You can have them back tomorrow.' The food was then brought to the table and he filled his nostrils with the inviting smell.

'Oh, wow!' said Ben as his eyes drank in the giant Yorkshire pudding before him. It was filled with sausages, vegetables and mashed potatoes. 'I have never seen anything like it,' he said as his mouth began to water.

The conversation ground to a halt as the sole focus became food. Knives were scraped across plates and forkfuls were shovelled into mouths until all the plates were pristinely clean. Hugh raised his arms above his head to stretch out his stomach. It was a feeble attempt to feel a little less full. He quickly lowered them again though as the weight of his stomach won the battle. Molly rested her elbows on the table and supported her head in her hands. 'I think I am going to give games a miss tonight,' she said, trying to stifle a yawn. 'I just want sleep.' Her blinking became slower and slower as her eyes tried to catch even a moment of rest.

'I think you speak for us all,' said Ally as her thoughts drifted towards the promise of a warm bed. In that moment, it was all she yearned for. Hugh slid off his chair. As he stood, he wobbled slightly from side to side. 'Please can we go?' he asked, pointing to the door.

'You guys get in the car and I'll settle up,' offered

Ben as he rose to his feet. He felt like his body had doubled in size! Ally, Hugh and Molly trudged their way out of the door, offering a brief wave to the bartender as they went. Ben slid the money across the bar. 'Thank you,' he said with sincerity. 'That was the best experience yet. And what are those things called that you filled with sausages again?' he asked.

'Yorkshire puddings,' answered the bartender with a smirk.

'Oh my! I am going to have to get some more of them,' declared Ben with a smile.

When they were all back in the car, Ally pulled out of the car park and headed back down the country road. It was now illuminated by starlight and she felt like the car was carrying them home. Every twist and turn in the road seemed to flow with ease. Molly stared up at the night sky. She had never seen so many stars before and she gently smiled to herself, for the first time in a very long time. She felt that she was being watched over and this brought with it such a sense of relief. Even when she couldn't see the stars she now knew that they were still there, to light her way.

Ally pulled up the gravel drive and parked outside the red front door, once again. She turned off the ignition and paused to listen to what most would say was silence. But for her, it was nature's music. The rustling leaves, the chirping crickets, the tweeting birds. It wasn't silent at all.

They all climbed out of the car, one by one, and stepped into the cottage. The lights illuminated the old stone. Molly and Hugh's feet were on railway tracks, heading in only one direction – their beds.

'Night,' said Hugh lazily and he vaguely wafted a hand in the air.

'Night, everyone,' mirrored Molly, as they disappeared up the stairs.

Ally placed her handbag down on the kitchen worktop and reached for the kettle. *One final cup of tea before bed*, she thought.

Ben leant against the worktop. His finger-tips ran along the edge of the post-it note that was still in his pocket.

'This place is like a fairy tale,' breathed Ally as she let her tea brew. She glanced across at Ben who was staring at the stone floor, deep in thought.

'What's got your attention?' Ally asked gently as she poured milk into her tea and threw away the bag.

'Oh, nothing,' replied Ben. 'It has been a hell of a couple of days. I think they are beginning to catch up with me, that's all,' he explained, trying to disguise the feeling of uncertainty building inside. Ally walked across with her cup of tea and leaned over to kiss him on the cheek. 'One day at a time,' she said. 'That's all we can do. Make the best of today but dream about tomorrow.'

Ben smiled and he allowed Ally's loving words to soothe the burning fire inside. 'I'll be up in a minute,' he said before kissing Ally on the lips. Ally glowed. Every kiss still felt like their first. She let her body buzz with joy as she made her way upstairs. Ben watched her as she went with a look of pure devotion in his eyes.

As soon as Ally had disappeared from view, Ben's body slumped forwards. He felt the last ounce of strength he was using to hold himself together, fade away. He slowly pulled the post-it note from his pocket and stared at the blankness. *When you realise you can have anything*, he thought. *You suddenly understand that you don't really know what you want.* He sighed. *No, that's not quite true*, he mused. *I do know what I want, but I've got responsibilities now. Can my own dreams still come true*? He closed his eyes and searched for guidance.

Ben found a pen on the worktop, walked back across the living room and out of the front door. He closed it silently behind him. He meandered over to the old oak tree, sat down and leant his back up against the trunk. The pen shook a little as it hovered over the post-it note. Thoughts began to flow through his mind. *I am here to live my life too. I may have new responsibilities, but I am not supposed to give up my life for others. Instead, we are meant to continue to live our own, individual lives, but intertwined with others of all ages.* 'Well, if that's the case then,' he said aloud, and he wrote his true heart's desire on the note. It was not what was expected of him, but what he wanted.

He bravely folded up the note and placed it in his jeans pocket. He let his head rest against the tree trunk and shut his eyes. He let the silence soothe his soul, and his breathing slowed. His body no longer felt restless, but at peace.

Ben felt a warmth on his skin and the smell of coffee around him. His eyelashes flickered as he opened his eyes and let them adjust to the morning light. His body felt stiff. 'Never quite made it up the stairs then?' said Ally softly. 'I was starting to get worried.'
'Oh boy,' yawned Ben. 'I must have dozed off.'
Ally smiled. 'You can't take the country out of a countryman. It's like a magnet always pulling him back. Come on. Hugh is making egg and bacon sandwiches,' she stated, raising her eyebrows,

feeling impressed.

'What no pancakes?' Ben asked. 'It must be a special day,' he added as Ally attempted to pull him up.

They stepped through the front door and were immediately hit by a wall of the glorious smell of bacon and fresh bread. 'Where have you guys been?' asked Hugh. 'Quick, breakfast is ready,' he ordered, wafting a spatula in the air.
'Is it me, or is he getting more demanding?' Ally questioned with a cheeky grin. They made their way over to the table and Ben sat down in front of his plate. He took the post-it note out of his pocket and slid it across to Hugh, but didn't feel able to make eye contact. Molly tilted her head to try and see what was written, but couldn't quite get the angle.

Hugh sank his teeth deep into the spongy, fresh bread, and melted butter seeped out of the corner of his mouth. 'Mmm,' he muttered, closing his eyes with pure delight. They all remained silent as, yet again, their full attention was captivated by and focused on their taste buds. Molly licked the end of her finger to pick up the last of the crumbs on her plate.
'Well, Hugh, you have outdone yourself this time,' complimented Ally as she surveyed the squeaky

clean plates.

'I'll do the washing up,' offered Molly and she started to collect the plates.

Hugh glanced at the clock on the wall. It was already 10am. He leapt to his feet. 'Come on, guys!' he cried. 'We best get a move on, otherwise we won't be able to spend all day at the waterfalls.'

'Monkey, don't worry,' soothed Ally. 'All we have to do is grab our coats, put on our shoes and we're ready. What's the hurry?' she asked, hoping for life to slow down, just a little. 'We have had an intense few days,' she added. 'Let's just take our feet off the accelerator a bit.'

'Yes, yes, Mom,' replied Hugh impatiently. 'We can do that when we're at the waterfalls.' Ally held his gaze, abruptly got up, picked up her handbag and coat, slipped on her shoes, grabbed the keys and stepped out of the front door. Hugh followed speedily behind her.

'But what about...?' asked Molly, holding up the plates.

'They will still be here when we get back,' replied Ben as he got up too. 'Come on. It looks like we're leaving.'

'I hope Hugh's wish was to receive patience,' Molly muttered.

Ben sniggered. 'You know Hugh! Why wait for

tomorrow if you can get it done today?'

Ben and Molly stepped out into the morning sun. There was a slight chill in the air. They made their way over to the car to join Ally and Hugh. Hugh reached forwards between the seats and turned on the radio. The lyrics '*Because I'm happpyyyy*,' filled the car and Hugh began to sing along. Ally couldn't help but smile. Hugh just didn't have a snooze button like the rest of them. It was always the right time to do something. She turned the steering wheel and rolled the car back onto the country roads.

The car glided as it weaved its way through the hillside. They found themselves climbing higher and higher, and Molly let out a secret smile. She felt a warmth in her heart beginning to glow. All that she had lost had been transformed. Not into something better, but something different. Something she yearned for and was ready to receive - a new dawn, a new beginning. They eventually entered a small village with old stone buildings clustered together. The narrow road only allowed one car through at a time. Ben's gaze darted around. It was like everything was in miniature, compared to what he was used to. Ally continued to follow the signs for the waterfall trail and her heart began to beat faster. Showing Ben into her world still unnerved her a little. Her worries fluttered inside. *What if this puts him off me? What if, after this trip, he doesn't want to marry me*? Ben suddenly took hold of her hand on the gear stick and gave it a reassuring squeeze, as if he had just read her mind.

'To think,' pondered Ben. 'If I hadn't met you, I wouldn't be seeing some of the most beautiful places on the planet!' he added with a huge smile.
Hugh began to wriggle in the back. Ally glanced at him in the rear-view mirror. 'I hope you know where we're going once we get on the trail?' she asked trustingly.
In true Hugh style, he pulled a map out of his rucksack. 'Mom, I have it covered.'
'Of course you do,' laughed Ally, shaking her head. Why did she even doubt him?

As they reached the entrance, they turned to the left and pulled into a parking space. 'Right, Hugh, lead the way,' Ally instructed as she turned off the ignition. She wanted to reach the waterfall quickly, so she could rest a while.
They all clambered out of the car. 'This way!' called Hugh over his shoulder as he marched on. Molly followed eagerly behind him.

Ben took hold of Ally's hand and intertwined his fingers with hers. They took a step forwards together, in perfect sync. The path began to climb up the hillside and they had to duck under the low-hanging branches. They could hear the gushing noise of the river below and as they stepped up onto a rock, they were treated to a view of it, in all its glory. The water bounced off the river bed as it flowed purposefully down. 'Come on,' said Hugh encouragingly. 'We're nearly at the first one.' He waved Ally and Ben on. 'The first one?' questioned Ally, a little out of breath, and a little unnerved. 'How many of them are there?'

'About 13 of them,' Hugh answered casually.

As they walked a little further, they started to feel the damp air whirl around their lungs, and a gentle mist of water began to appear. They had reached the first waterfall. Ben moved behind Ally and wrapped his arms around her waist. He rested his head on her shoulder and they all took a moment to admire the hypnotic flow of the water. It cascaded and fell freely over the rocks, and then crashed onto the river bed below. The noise of the tumbling water echoed around the valley that it had carved out, over thousands of years. But still, Mother Nature continued to adapt. New trees were beginning to grow on the valley sides, to take the place of the old, fallen down ones.

Ben drew in the air, lifted his finger and pointed. 'Look,' he whispered. 'It's us. Two waterfalls becoming one.' They traced the path of two streams coming together from different directions and forming the waterfall.

Ally snuggled in closer to him. 'You never doubt our love, or what is going to be, do you?' she asked in awe.

'Not with you,' answered Ben with conviction. 'I have heard a few men speak of a love like the kind I feel for you. But they always said it was the scariest choice they ever made - to love so deeply, so purely and unconditionally. Because they knew how much they had to lose in order to gain so much. But all of them said it was the best choice they ever made and that they don't regret it for one day. Yet, they said that most of those they speak to about a love so pure, never truly get it. It is only when you are loved unconditionally do you truly understand what love is.'

Ben stepped around Ally and continued down the path. Hugh and Molly had already gone ahead. 'Hey!' Ally called after him. 'Thank you for being so brave.' She smiled with admiration.

'I didn't have a choice,' replied Ben. 'I just let my heart be my compass.'

Ally scurried to Ben's side. *Always together*, she

thought. *Hand in hand, side by side.*

As they walked over the next ridge, the landscape opened up into a wide, open valley of fields, and there in the centre, was the base of a waterfall. Ally gasped in wonder at the sheer beauty. There were no words.

'Oh, he is good,' said Ben, smiling like a child on Christmas morning. Both he and Ally ran playfully down to the water's edge. Hugh and Molly were already there, crouched down. Ally and Ben watched as Hugh and Molly each took a leaf and placed their post-it note inside. They were folded into the smallest square they could possibly make. Ben and Ally joined them, took their post-it notes from Hugh and also placed them in a leaf that Molly had collected for them.

They lined up all four of the leaves in the still water at the edge. 'Ready?' Molly asked.

'Ready,' confirmed Ben, Ally and Hugh in unison. They gently pushed their leaves and watched them glide away. The leaves were soon caught by the current and they twisted and turned, and bobbed up and down on the water's surface, and down towards their destinations.

The four of them watched as Mother Nature transported their heart's desires to the place

where they would be fulfilled and come true.
'Thank you, Hugh,' said Molly, hugging him tightly.
'I needed to do that more than I knew,' she
added gratefully.
'I think we were all ready to dream again,'
responded Hugh. 'After great loss comes great
abundance. As long as you remember to ask,' he
added as he ran his fingertips through the cool,
crystal-clear water. This simple movement started
to turn up the volume on his thoughts about faith,
and pressed the mute button on his fears.

Molly stared at her reflection in the water. It
rippled for a while and then became still. She
looked at the waterfall towering over her in the
background. Thousands of gallons of water leapt
bravely off the edge. She shivered as a cool
breeze whirled around her, and lifted wisps of her
hair. Molly stared yet harder still at the waterfall,
and began to feel the power and force, and the
sound of the water hitting the rocks, like a
heartbeat. All that had been and all that was
meant to be, seemed so insignificant, so small
against the waterfall. Her fears were just the
water droplets, but her dreams were the
waterfall. 'It's all relative,' she whispered. 'It's my
choice whether I make my dreams bigger, or my
fears.'

Something caught her attention out of the corner

of her eye. She turned to see a black feather floating towards her. Ben reached forwards and picked it up. 'I think this may be for you,' he said, handing it across to Molly.

Molly took it and held it up to the sunlight. She could see flickers of blue and green in the feather. 'That's not good,' she said with concern. 'It's not white.'

Ben stood up. 'Anyone can have faith when things are going well and life is full of light,' he said. 'But it takes courage, and a lot of heart to still believe when you are surrounded by the darkness, yet are still able to feel and know the truth' he concluded. He continued along the path, followed by Ally and Hugh.

5 LOCHS OF LUCK

Molly slowly rose to her feet and tucked the feather in her pocket. She would add it to her tin owl box when she got back. They continued to walk along the trail. There was a buzz running between them, a warmth. Just for this moment in time they were enjoying the fact that everything was perfect. Nobody needed anything more. The feeling of true fulfilment was inescapable.

Hugh and Molly bounded ahead like two excited deer. Ben walked proudly behind with Ally's arm casually draped across his. They let Mother Nature do what she does best, her presence soothing and softening their hearts, strengthening their souls and lightening their load. Hugh and Molly stopped at the next small waterfall, slipped off their shoes and dipped their toes into the water. There was a sudden yelp as they jumped back. 'Ooh, that's cold!' Molly cried, shaking her body. But, she carefully stepped back into the water. Her feet slowly became numb as she moved further in, until it was just above her ankles.

Hugh quickly put his socks and shoes back on. 'I think I'll watch this one,' he said with a smirk. Molly closed her eyes and let the feeling of the water roll over her toes. With every passing moment, she felt relief rise up from her feet and travel all the way to the top of her head. Her body relaxed enough to allow her to take her first deep breath in days. But, her eyes suddenly flipped open. 'So, where next on your map, Hugh?' she called.
Hugh was slightly taken by surprise as he, too, was lost in his own thoughts.

Hugh's smile quickly grew. 'If you thought this was good,' he said teasingly. 'Wait until you see where we're heading to next.'
Molly felt a flutter of excitement in her stomach. 'Well, what are we waiting for?' she said, skipping out of the water and quickly putting on her socks and shoes.
Ally stopped a moment, pulled Ben back and stared warily across at Hugh and Molly. 'Oh no,' she groaned. 'I know that look.'
Ben followed her gaze. 'What look?' he asked, a

little puzzled. 'That look,' said Ally. She was pointing at Hugh who was sprinting towards them with Molly.

Ally remained silent as she waited for the next tidal wave of change.

'What have you just thought of?' asked Ben as Hugh skidded to a halt. His curiosity had become too strong to stay silent.

'Well,' responded Hugh. 'I think it's time to move onto the next step of our journey,' he said, his hands clasped behind his back. Molly stood patiently behind him.

'Yes, no problem,' said Ally. 'We'll set off in the morning,' she added casually before taking a step forward.

But, Hugh stepped in front of her and blocked her path. He shook his head from side to side. Ally really was confused now. 'In a couple of days then?' she asked, still not convinced. Hugh continued to shake his head. 'Monkey! Would you just tell me,' Ally said, clearly frustrated. Hugh shook his head from side to side again. 'Tonight then,' Ally said angrily.

'What a great idea, Mom,' he said calmly. 'Let's head back and pack up the car.' With that, he turned on his heels and continued along the path to the car park.

Ally scowled. 'I love that child more than life itself, and would do anything for him, but I don't always like him,' she admitted truthfully.

Ben wrapped his arm around her and squeezed her tightly. 'Now that is parenting,' he said simply. They continued down the path and soon reached the car park. Molly and Hugh were already standing, patiently by the door.

Ally smiled mischievously as she got closer to the car. 'Come on, Mom! Open up. I want to get in,' Hugh ordered impatiently.

Ally winked at Ben. 'Oh no!' she said with mock alarm. 'I think I've lost the keys.' She patted her pockets and glanced dramatically behind her, up the trail.

Hugh's face dropped with disappointment.

'What?' he asked in shock.

'I am sure I gave them to you, Ben,' said Ally calmly.

'Nope,' said Ben, enjoying the game. 'You definitely had them.'

'Well, where the devil are they?' Ally queried with her hands on her hips. 'We best retrace our steps,' she said decidedly.

'You must be joking,' groaned Hugh. 'Please tell me she's joking.' He was becoming more and more agitated, but surrendered to the idea and began to make his way back up the trail. But there was a sudden click and a flash of lights behind him. Hugh paused and looked back at Ally, who was standing by the unlocked car, swinging her keys from her finger. Hugh was slightly impressed with her prank, but wasn't going to tell her that, obviously. 'Alright, I get the message,' he said with resignation and climbed into the car.

'Like Grandma always said,' responded Ally, quite pleased with herself. 'Let life provide the consequences and the lessons.' They all climbed back into the car and retraced their steps down the country road. Each time the red door of the cottage came into view, it was that little bit more familiar.
Hugh thought about his lesson. 'What would everybody like to do next?' he asked. He was beginning to understand that they were all on this journey together.

'Well I for one, am starving!' exclaimed Molly. 'So, food first,' she said determinedly as she patted her stomach.
'Then pack up and hit the road again,' added Ally, looking at Hugh and smiling at him.
Hugh began to feel more settled as they pulled up in front of the red door. 'I'll make a start on

some food,' offered Ben. 'Do we still have the basket full of food?' he inquired.

'Yeah, in the boot,' Ally said apprehensively.

Ben stepped out the car. Ally turned in her seat and was about to say something, but she stopped herself. 'Never mind,' she said, shaking her head, and she headed into the cottage.

'Come on, let's go and pack our bags,' Molly said, trying to reignite Hugh's passion.

'I don't mean to be bossy,' he said feeling a little ashamed.

Molly playfully pushed him. 'We need you to be,' she said reassuringly. 'We wouldn't get anything done otherwise. Hey, don't you start going all soft on me,' she warned, playfully wiggling her finger at him.

Hugh smiled. 'Last one to the door has to wash up!'

Molly's eyes widened with fear. She hated washing up, so quickly darted as fast as she could to the front door.

Hugh and Molly ran through the living room where Ben was already preparing some food, and Ally was setting the table. They dashed into their bedroom and hurriedly packed away their belongings.

'Food's ready!' called Ben. Hugh and Molly

grabbed their suitcases, put them beside the
front door and joined Ally and Ben at the table.

'This looks delicious,' Ally said as she breathed in
the aroma.
'Before we start,' said Ben. 'I think now would be
a good time to say what we're thankful for.'
Molly looked disappointed. Her stomach rumbled
with excitement at the sight of the feast in front
of her. 'I am thankful for family and making a
wish today' she blurted out. 'Your turn, Hugh,' she
said hurriedly, trying to speed up the process.
She sneaked a fork full into her mouth.
'I am grateful for being able to explore and make
new memories,' answered Hugh as he glanced
across to Ally.
'I am grateful for unconditional love and second
chances,' said Ally as she took hold of Ben's
hand.
'I am grateful for good friends who are taking
care of the ranch, and the chance to spend time
with the 3 most important people in my life,'
concluded Ben.

'Great,' cried Molly with relief. 'Let's eat!' She
celebrated by shovelling the first mouthful
in...well, the second. Her taste buds danced with
delight. The room remained silent as they all
devoured their food. The silence around them

serenaded their meal.

Hugh was the first to get up and he walked around the table, collecting everyone's plates. 'Oh thanks, Hugh. That's so kind of you to do the washing up,' exclaimed Molly wishfully.

'Ha! Not a chance,' replied Hugh. 'Me and you are doing this while Mom and Ben pack.' Hugh glanced out of the window and noticed that dusk had arrived. He watched the stars take centre stage. It was their time to shine now.

Ben and Ally got up and disappeared into the bedroom to collect their belongings. Molly filled up the kitchen sink and started to wash the first pots. 'Tell me more about the next place, Hugh,' Molly asked with a smile. She felt excitement in her tummy, something she hadn't realised had been missing in her life recently.

'Well, it's called The Lochs of Luck,' replied Hugh. 'It sounds like *lots of luck* when you say it out loud,' he chuckled.

Molly scrunched up her nose. 'But we don't need luck,' she stated. 'We can achieve anything.'

'Luck isn't that random thing that just happens to a few people,' explained Hugh. 'Luck is the chance to find or acquire something,' he continued.

Molly handed Hugh a plate to dry. 'What is it that you want to find?' she asked, her confusion now piquing as curiosity.

'I don't know,' uttered Hugh. 'I am hoping I will find out when we get there. Sometimes, we don't know something is missing until life gives it to us and we're reminded.'

They were interrupted by the sound of Ally and Ben opening the front door and taking the bags out to the car. They both looked at each other and wiggled with joy. Hugh put the last plate away and hung up the tea towel. 'Come on!' he cried. 'Let's get in the car.' And they both ran as fast as they could towards their next adventure.

Ben glanced around the cottage one last time, pulled the front door closed and locked it. Ally started up the engine and turned on the head lights. A dark cloak of night, with little speckles of light, was spread across the sky. The full moon shone brightly and illuminated the valley sides, painting a perfect picture: a moonscape. The land looked soft and still. Mother Nature was resting after another busy day of hard work. Hugh stared out of the window. *I have never seen the land look so magical*, he thought to himself with a smile.

He rolled up his coat and placed it against the window – a makeshift pillow. He let his head rest against it. 'Maybe the dark nights have their own kind of beauty,' he said.

'I agree,' said Molly. 'There is something mysterious about the countryside at night, and a calmness. But yet, a sort of knowing.' She glanced across at Hugh and then copied his coat-pillow with her own. She felt the relief carry the weight of her thoughts.

Ben climbed in and closed the door behind him. Ally pulled away from the cottage and began to navigate the car along the country roads, once more, and then onto the motorway. But this time, there were no other cars in sight. Just the occasional lorry on its own journey, which passed by every once in a while.

Ally wriggled in her seat to try and relieve the numbness in her bottom. She glanced in the rear-view mirror to see that Molly and Hugh had already fallen fast asleep. 'Well, that didn't take long,' she said. But her comment was met with silence. She looked across and saw that Ben had fallen asleep too. Ally smiled. 'I guess it's just me then,' she said to nobody in particular as she continued to coast along the open road. For the first time since arriving back in England, she was alone with her thoughts. She felt her grip tighten on the wheel and her arms brace, ready for the barrage of fears, tears and failures. But her mind remained silent as she continued to watch the bright light of the moon illuminate the road ahead of her.

Ally felt her grip loosen and her arms begin to relax. 'Can everything really be alright?' she asked herself quietly, and suddenly found herself smiling. 'Yes, yes, it is,' she confirmed and pressed her foot harder against the accelerator. She let the feeling of freedom take hold. She got lost in the drive as she steered the car higher and higher up the country, and the hours seamlessly rolled on by. At some point, Ally glanced at the clock. It was 4am. She watched the full moon lower itself in front of her and the sun begin to rise behind. Life was suspended in time, between night and day, as the sun tried to playfully catch the moon.

Ally took in a deep breath. How could a moment this spectacular be seen and admired by so few? In a couple of hours' time, alarm clocks would be waking everybody and they would be starting the morning rush to work or school. They would be too busy to catch such a moment. Has life really got any easier, or just quicker? Ally began to wonder.

Ben slowly lifted his head. He rubbed his neck and let out a low groan as his muscles began to readjust. 'Morning, Sleepy,' said Ally.
Ben looked ahead to see the last part of the

moon disappear behind the horizon. He glanced down at the clock. 'Hmm,' he said lazily. 'That was some sleep.' He looked across at Ally. 'Are you alright?' he asked. 'You've been driving for some time now. Maybe we should stop and pick up a coffee.'

Ally drove straight past a sign for a Service Station. 'No, I am fine,' she replied. 'I just want to get there now.' Her eyes were fixed on the road ahead.

'Ally, my wonderful Ally,' sang Ben. 'But, I really need to pee!'

Ally shot Ben a look. 'Oh well, OK then. A short break won't hurt,' she acknowledged as she swerved the car down the slip road, towards the services.

Ally pulled into a car parking space and opened the door. A wave of fresh air washed across her face. It seemed purer somehow, and cleaner. She felt herself emerge from her driving trance as she stretched out her legs. They took some coaxing out of their new programmed driving position.

'Shall we wake them?' Ben asked over the roof of the car. They peered through the window. Molly was now asleep on Hugh's shoulder and Hugh had his head resting on hers.

'No, I think they will need all the sleep they can get,' answered Ally. 'But you're on first shift when we get there, while I catch up on my sleep,' she instructed.

'Deal,' agreed Ben, quietly closing the car door before making their way across to the services.

Hugh felt himself drift awake and then sink back into sleep again as he hovered in the space of dreams. He watched the pictures as they floated through his mind. The colours were so bright and vivid, that he almost felt as if he could touch them. They seemed so real. He found himself smiling at the image of him holding a trophy up, above his head. But as he tried to focus on the engraving, he became confused. It didn't say *Roping Champion* on it. It said the word *Family*. His thoughts became momentarily scrambled, but then relief washed over him. He had never let himself believe that he could be part of a family again. But the piece of himself that had gone up to the stars, with his dad, now floated back down and returned to his heart.

Hugh's eyelids flickered as he saw morning sunlight sparkling on the leaves of a hedgerow. The car had stopped and they were in a car park. He felt the reassuring weight of Molly's head on his shoulder. While no one was looking, he let out a tear. Not of sadness, but one of pure joy. The dream he thought would never come true, the dream he didn't dare to dream, had come true. 'I guess I underestimated a wish from the heart,' he said quietly to himself as he wrapped his arms around Molly and squeezed her so tightly. He wanted to fit all of her in his arms and not leave a single cell out.

Hugh heard the familiar voices of Ally and Ben as they made their way back across to the car. He listened to his mom's laughter, which always felt like a river of gold washing over his body. Hugh slowly released his grip on Molly, closed his eyes and pretended to be asleep.

Ally climbed in first and Ben quickly followed. 'Could you pass me the map, please,' she said, as she placed her coffee cup on the dashboard. Ben passed it to her and she traced the single road that led to Hugh's post-it note. 'You know, we should be there in a couple of hours,' she said gladly. Her bottom was still numb from the previous hours.
'Just in time for breakfast,' replied Ben, rubbing his stomach. Ally placed the key in the ignition and the engine came back to life. She began to drive out of the car park.

Hugh listened to the hum of Ben and Ally's conversation as he watched out of the window. The hills were growing bigger as the road cut through the valley. There wasn't another car in sight. The sky was bright blue, like sapphire, with just a pink tinge as the sun continued to rise higher. He sat, motionless, simply savouring the moment. He didn't want Ally to see this truth. He had hidden his heart's longing from her for so long. This had been just a dream for him, and now, without even knowing it, she had helped to make it come true.

The road began to narrow as it shrunk from motorway to country road. Hugh shuffled. His arm had officially gone numb from the weight of Molly and he gently pushed her back against her window. He felt a hand on his knee. 'Morning, Monkey. Welcome to paradise,' greeted Ally. Hugh poked his head through the gap in the front seats. The road glided seamlessly along the edge of the loch, which was a perfect mirror of the sky and land surrounding it.

Ally slowed down as they reached a T-junction. As she turned right, a white hotel came into view. 'I think here might be a good place as any to stay for a night or two,' she said with relief. She would be glad to give the driving a break for a while. She pulled into the car park and turned off the engine. They all sat in silence and awe, looking out across the vast loch. 'I have never seen anything so beautiful,' breathed Ally, breaking the quiet.

To the left, they could see a large hill. Little streams carved their way through the land, like veins, trickling down to the loch. To the right was a large steep bank covered with a forest and a road going along the water's edge. The water lay motionless, a crystal-clear mirror reflecting the bright blue sky and the sun, which had slowly begun to rise. The land was beginning to wake.

Hugh was the first to clamber out of the car. He took a huge breath in. The air felt different, cleaner and more pure. He walked to the water's edge and knelt down. He formed a cup with his hands, scooped up a handful of water and splashed his face. He felt the crisp, clean water run over his face and fingers, and something deep inside began to dissolve away. The untouchable darkness that had been lingering in the background, controlling his choices, was now gone. He stared at his reflection in the crystal-clear water. It was like a looking glass to a secret world and he began to remember, a truth once forgotten had now returned.

Ally and Ben approached the entrance of the hotel and Ben wrapped his arm around Ally's waist, pulling her in close. They scanned the landscape, a picture that truly was beyond words. They felt humbled to be part of something so awe-inspiring. Hugh's approaching footsteps

behind them brought them out of their trance.
'Well done, Monkey,' congratulated Ally. 'This is one incredible dream you are sharing with us all.' She pulled him in for a hug.

The car door then slammed and a very sleepy Molly staggered her way across to where they were all standing. 'What did I miss?' she asked, rubbing her eyes.

'Breakfast, lunch and dinner,' replied Hugh with a smirk.

Molly pretended to look shocked. 'No, really, what did I miss?' she asked. 'Hang on a minute. You look different, Hugh,' she queried as her eyes scanned him up and down. 'I can't quite put my finger on it. But something has changed.'

Hugh looked down at his feet and shuffled them against the step. He felt his cheeks begin to redden.

'Hugh?' said Ally. 'Is there something you're not telling us?' She peered down at him.

'Yes, actually. Yes, there is,' answered Hugh. They all waited with baited breath. 'I am starving!' he shouted after a long pause.

Ally instantly relaxed. 'Well, it's a good job they have started to serve breakfast,' she said with a smile as she and Ben headed into the hotel.

Molly marched past Hugh with an obvious scowl on her face. She was not convinced that was the thing that was different.

'Good morning,' greeted a young gentleman with a smile.

'Could we have a table for four please,' asked Ben.

'Of course. Come this way,' said the waiter. He turned to make his way across the old, oak wooden floor. His shiny black shoes clicked as he walked. They all followed and took a seat at the table that he gestured towards. The waiter began to hand out the menus, but Ally lifted up her hand to stop him. 'I'll make this easy for you,' she said. 'Four cooked breakfasts, with everything on it please.'

The waiter was slightly disappointed that he couldn't run through his usual speech but politely collected the menus. 'Of course, Mam,' he said formally, before, once again, clicking his way across the floor.

Molly became lost in her thoughts as she looked out of the window. 'That's it!' she suddenly cried, slamming her hand down on the table. It made Ally jump and drop her cutlery onto the floor. Molly turned her focus to Hugh. 'You have been to down to the loch,' she said. 'You have got your luck back! Did you make another wish? Was it good? What does it feel like?' she blurted out.

Hugh sat in stunned silence for a moment, feeling a little dazed. 'Umm, well,' he began, trying to fit his answer in between Molly's endless questions. He finally gave in and placed his hand across her mouth. 'If you would just be quiet for a minute,' he instructed. 'I will tell you.' Molly only managed to give him a moment before the next impatient question was about to burst out of her mouth. 'Actually, I'm not going to tell you,' said Hugh teasingly. 'You can find out for yourself.'

Hugh lifted his hand off Molly's mouth and she paused. *It's not like Hugh to be stuck for words*, she thought.

'Well, if you won't tell me what you discovered, then at least explain to us what the heck we are doing here,' Molly ordered, becoming frustrated.

'Language, young lady,' Ally said, raising her eyebrows in warning.

'Sorry,' muttered Molly.

Hugh took the map out of his pocket and laid it in the centre of the table. 'Try and listen this time,' he said. 'See these pools of water? Well they are like large wells of luck, surrounded by the land. Hence the name, Lochs of Luck.'

Molly crinkled her nose. 'Why do we need luck?' she asked again, still unable to grasp what Hugh was talking about.

Hugh looked across at Ben for a bit of help. His previous explanation obviously hadn't sunk in.

'Well, most people think that luck is just random,' explained Ben. 'Something good that happens by chance. But there is another truth to luck. It is actually the chance to find or acquire something,' he continued.

'What, like gold?' questioned Molly. 'Not that I need any,' she quickly added, feeling a little bashful.

'Luck can come in many different forms,' Ben further clarified. 'Yes, it could be things, or it could be an experience. It could be avoiding a problem or a problem being easily solved. It can be finding out something new about yourself. Luck takes whatever form you need it to take, to continue to have faith, and believe in life's truths and your dreams.'

Molly sat back in her chair and Hugh began to play with his napkin. 'Like me finding my self-belief,' he whispered.

Ben and Ally glanced at each other as they all fell into silence.

'When Dad went, I felt a piece of me go with him to the stars,' said Hugh. 'And now I know it was the part of me that believed in myself. That's what I have been searching for. I can't explain it, but when I looked into that water, it was like I was looking straight into a part of myself that I don't get to see every day. And then I just felt it, a piece slot back into me, like a jigsaw. I don't know, maybe it was my imagination,' he said, pushing his napkin away.

'Well, if you felt it and I saw it, then it's true,' Molly replied confidently, knocking Hugh's doubts away.

Molly wrapped her arms around Hugh's neck. 'Welcome home, Hugh's self-belief,' she whispered. But she pulled back when they heard the welcome clatter of plates being placed on the table. 'After breakfast,' she stated. 'I am going to find...' She paused thoughtfully before continuing. 'Whatever it is that I am meant to find.' She smiled and shoved a large piece of egg into her mouth. The yolk dripped down her chin and everybody laughed. The atmosphere was relaxing once more.

A short while later, the waiter returned to the table. He surveyed the plates. 'Well, I'm glad you all left the pattern on the plates, at least. You must have been hungry! Have you travelled far?' he asked amiably as he balanced the plates into a perfect stack on his arm.

'We've only travelled for a few hours,' replied Molly.

'And the rest,' corrected Ally. 'You were asleep for the other few.'

Molly playfully stuck her tongue out at Ally.

'Is there anything else I can get you?' asked the waiter. 'Yes, a pot of tea for me please,' asked Ally. 'To take up to our room.' Her eyelids were now needing mini-sticks to keep them open.
'I'll have it sent up,' said the waiter sympathetically. Ally gave him a thankful smile. She looked across at Ben. 'A deal is a deal,' she reminded him.
Ben looked sheepish. He was hoping she might have forgotten. 'Not a chance,' Ally said, reading his thoughts. She tapped the side of her head and winked at him, before standing up.

'I'm going to catch up on some sleep,' she explained. 'You guys have fun and I'll see you in a couple of hours.' She made her way back through to reception and Ben leant on the table.
'OK, you two. What have you got in mind?' he asked with a cheeky look on his face.
'Let's climb up through the forest,' Hugh suggested.
'And let's go and walk around the loch,' Molly added.
'Hmm, how about we find a boat and go out to that island, where we can do both?' Ben suggested gleefully. Molly and Hugh's eyes widened and glistened with excitement. 'Excuse

me,' called Ben, trying to catch the waiter's attention.

The waiter wound his way back to their table.

'Yes, Sir,' he asked.

'Any chance you know where we might be able to hire a boat for a few hours?' asked Ben.

'Ah, yes. Just head back down the road for 10 minutes and you'll see John's place on your left. He'll be able to sort you out,' explained the waiter helpfully.

'Thank you,' they all said in unison as they began to get up from their seats.

'Right, you guys get your coats and I'll go and tell Ally,' said Ben. He looked through the doorway and saw Ally dragging herself heavily up the stairs. 'On second thoughts,' he pondered. 'We'll let her know when we get back.' They all headed to the car. Hugh was the first to dive into the boot and he eagerly pulled out their coats. Molly took Ben's hand and Hugh reached across and took the other as they crossed the road and began their walk to John's place.

Molly looked down and saw that their feet were stepping in time as they strode along the water's edge. Their eyes darted around as they absorbed the colours of the leaves and the ripples on the water, which moved with the gentle breeze. Molly quickened her pace as the anticipation grew. Ben's arm became stretched out in front of him. 'I

see it, I see it!' she cried, letting go of his hand and running down a driveway. There was a small cabin and a jetty, lined with boats.
'Wait for me!' shouted Hugh as he ran after her.

Ben lengthened his stride to keep up with them. He approached the cabin and pushed the front door open. The bell rang to herald a new arrival. Molly and Hugh were already peering over the counter. 'Morning, Sir,' greeted Ben as he held his hand out to a man he assumed was John. John reached back and shook it. 'These two were saying you're in need of a boat for a couple of hours, to head to the islands?' he inquired.
'Yes, that's correct,' replied Ben, glancing down at Hugh and Molly who were hopping excitedly from one foot to the other.
'Aye, you two best go and get yourselves a life jacket, and one for your dad too.'

Hugh and Molly dashed into the next room which was lined with life jackets of different shapes and sizes. They chose two that looked about right and put them on. They grabbed a larger one for Ben and headed back to the counter. The bell rang again as John walked out of the front door. 'This way then,' he called behind him and they all made their way outside and along the jetty. They could hear the wood creaking beneath their feet.

'Here you go then,' said John. 'Boat number 11 is ready.' Ben got in first. He took a moment to balance his body against the wobbles before helping Molly in, and then Hugh. 'Alright then,' said John. 'Have a good time and I'll be in the shop if you need anything.' He pulled his collar around his neck to shelter from the cold and disappeared back along the jetty.

'We will,' acknowledged Ben. He took his baseball cap out of his coat pocket and slipped it on. 'Right, you two. Can you sit on that bench for me?' he asked as he clambered over to the back of the boat, where the engine was. It caused the boat to wobble and rock again.
'Agh!' cried Molly as she gripped onto the seat. 'Oh, don't be such a diva, Molly,' Hugh said sarcastically. He was hoping that nobody saw him take a tighter grip on the seat as well.

Ben pulled the cord and the engine roared into life. 'Ready, you guys?' he shouted above the noise.
'Ready!' they both cried excitedly. Ben steered the boat easily away from the jetty and out into open water. Molly's hair flew behind her as they motored their way across to an island. The breeze had disappeared so the water was still again. Hugh took a deep breath and Molly let out a squeal of excitement as she felt a new sense of

freedom. Ben's eyes stayed focused on the shore of the island up ahead.

Earlier that morning, at breakfast, they had all gazed out of the window at a tiny dot-island on the horizon. They now watched that very island grow larger and larger as Ben navigated the boat towards it. They could see the detail of the trees and the rocks, and a pebble shoreline. Ben eased his hand off the throttle and the boat began to slow. It glided towards the edge and they heard a gentle crunch as the bottom of the boat rubbed against the pebbles on the loch bed. Ben slipped off his shoes and socks, rolled up his trousers and stepped into the water. He pulled at the rope at the front of the boat and tied it to a nearby tree.

He held out his hand and guided both Molly and Hugh onto the shore. 'Wow! This place is magical,' breathed Hugh as he gazed up at the canopy of trees. Ben wriggled out of his life jacket and helped Molly and Hugh with theirs. They left them in the boat and began to make their way towards the middle of the island.

They could hear the sound of twigs breaking under their feet as they walked further onto the island. The echo of the twig-snaps echoed through the trees. 'It's so peaceful here,' Molly whispered, but she felt that even a whisper was too loud for this mesmerising place. She heard a sound in the distance and veered off to the left, to follow both the noise and a growing feeling inside. She took hold of the locket in her fingers and knew, instinctively, that she was being guided towards something. She walked around a group of trees, and the land suddenly opened up to a pool of water lined with rocks. Molly carefully made her way down. The moss felt like carpet underneath her as she knelt by the water's edge.

Molly stared into the clear water, to the very bottom of the pool. 'Oh my!' she sighed. 'I have never before seen water so pure.' Her focus then shifted as she saw her reflection in the water-mirror. Her hair was falling down by the sides of her face and she reached up to tuck it behind her ears. She looked into her own eyes. She had never seen them shine so brightly. The locket dropped through her fingers and swung from her neck, in perfect time to the gentle breeze. Molly gasped for air. The soft wind began to shift the leaves on the trees and a beam of sunlight seeped through and illuminated the locket. Molly watched in awe as the light bounced off it, making it shine like a star. Her gaze softened with a knowing, an understanding of a truth. She felt her whole body become warm as each muscle relaxed, and she sensed something rising from deep within. It was shining and glowing, a new life

which was just about to begin. Molly ran her
fingers through the water and caused it to ripple.
She watched her reflection wiggle and move
before the water became still once more. When
she refocused, she could see that something
within her had been reborn.

Ben glanced across to see Molly kneeling by the
water's edge, and couldn't stop a smile creeping
across his face. Just then, he felt his coat pocket
vibrate, and he reached inside to pull out his
phone. He glanced down to see that he had
received a new message. It was from Ally: *We
have received the adoption certificate. We are
now, officially, a family of 4. A xx.* Ben glanced
back at Molly. 'Is my daughter there?' he shouted
with sheer delight.
Molly's head shot up. 'What did he just say?' she
whispered. As the words slowly filtered through
her mind and turned into realisation, she jumped
to her feet. She ran up to Ben, as fast as she
could, and flung her arms around him. He pulled
her up into his arms and held her tightly. They
gently swung from side to side as they celebrated
this brand new start.

6 OPENING PANDORA'S BOX

Ben, Molly and Hugh continued to climb higher, making new footprints in a place unknown. Molly skipped ahead, alive with the news that Ben had just shared with her through Ally's text. Hugh clambered up the nearest rock. 'Hello down there!' he called before jumping off.
They twirled around the trees, laughing and exploring, revelling in the sense of freedom their new truths gave them. Molly leapt deftly over a fallen tree and paused a moment, in thought. 'Have you found your luck yet, Ben?' she asked as her curiosity pondered what it might be.

Ben pulled himself over the log, jumped up and grabbed onto a nearby branch. He paused a moment and then let his body swing back and forth, completely in tune with his inner child. 'Not yet, Molly,' he replied. 'But when I do, you'll be the first to know.' He swung past her, like a monkey.

Molly didn't move. 'Ben?' she continued.

Ben let go of the branch and his feet made a soft thud on the ground. 'Yes, Molly?' he said, feeling the continued heat from the interrogation.

'You have everything figured out,' mused Molly. 'And you're very wise. Maybe you don't need to find anything.' She placed her hands on her hips with presumed authority.

Ben's gaze drifted to the view through the trees. 'Molly,' he said assertively. 'I most certainly have not got things figured out. And there is always more wisdom to acquire. I too have things I need to heal. But, the longer I can put off having to open Pandora's Box, the better.' He heard his words as he spoke them out loud and felt disappointed with himself. He hadn't voiced it like that before. Well, not openly anyway.

Hugh came and perched on a nearby rock. 'Is it anything we can help with?' he asked with concern.

'I guess if I could have a few hours alone with your mom, that would help,' replied Ben. 'I think I need to tell her something. Not for her sake, but for mine. I don't want to be carrying the past with me into my future,' he added, fighting back the tears.

'You could practise telling us first,' Molly suggested. She tried to sound calm but she was dying to know what was inside Ben's Pandora's Box.

Ben smiled knowingly. 'I bet you would like that,' he said. 'But, this is a conversation for me and Ally. If I want my wish to come true, then I need to cut a cord from the past that is holding me back.'

'In that case,' said Hugh. 'Let's go and drop the boat off at John's, and head back to the hotel. Me and Molly can play in the hotel living room while you and mom talk,' he suggested with urgency.

'No, there's no need to rush,' replied Ben. 'Let's explore some more.' He knew, deep down, that he was stalling for time. He kind of wished he hadn't said anything at all now.

'Boat, now!' ordered Molly, pointing determinedly back the way they had come.

Ben stuck his bottom lip out and dragged his feet along the ground. 'You can be so bossy sometimes,' he said, pretending to sulk like a child. He put his thumb to his nose and wiggled his fingers, mockingly, before sprinting back to the boat. Hugh and Molly leapt and bound behind him and they all started to laugh.

'I win,' cried Ben playfully, holding his hands up in

the air, like a champion.

'Aren't you supposed to let us win?' said Molly, climbing into the boat and giving him a look. Hugh scrambled in next, followed by Ben and they all put their life jackets back on. Molly wriggled and fidgeted, and then suddenly screamed, 'yahoo!' It felt as if she would burst with happiness if she didn't let it out.

'Someone is glad to find their luck,' giggled Hugh. Ben started up the engine and pulled away from the shore. Molly felt a little more settled having got it off her chest. 'Oh, Hugh! I so get it now,' she said, squeezing his arm with delight.

Ben drove the boat more slowly on the way back. He felt that he would have to delve into his darkest secrets the second he stepped back onto the jetty: *Maybe I don't need to tell her. Maybe I just need to never think of it again.* He tried to seek comfort in his own thoughts and find an exit out of the uncomfortable feeling that was taking hold inside.

The jetty approached all too quickly. They saw John appear from around the side of the cabin and make his way down towards the empty space on the jetty. 'Hugh,' said Ben. 'When we get close enough, can you throw John that rope so that he can secure it to the jetty?'

Hugh carefully edged towards the front of the

boat. He felt a little uneasy and tried to push down mental pictures of the boat capsizing. 'Ready!' he shouted when he was in place. Ben began to slow the boat and directed it seamlessly into its place. Hugh threw the rope with all his might. John snapped up the end and tied it to the metal ring on the jetty.

John held out his hand and Hugh grabbed hold. He pulled himself back onto land, and felt his legs wobble, as if he was still on the boat. Molly was the next out and she linked arms with Hugh when she joined him on the jetty. Ben casually stepped out of the boat. 'Awesome,' he said to John, his voice alive with enthusiasm.
'So, you found what you were searching for?' asked John, looking down at Molly and Hugh.
'Absolutely,' confirmed Molly, high-fiving him with just a little too much clout. John rubbed his hand quickly on his side to take away the sting. He hoped nobody saw.

'What are you up to?' Hugh asked as he peeked around the side of the cabin.
'Oh, just giving boat number 4 a bit of love,' replied John. 'They need taking care of and nurturing, otherwise they would fall apart.'
'Can we help?' Molly asked bluntly and automatically picked up the paint brush.

John glanced across at Ben, looking for permission. Ben shrugged his shoulders. 'It's alright with me,' he confirmed. 'But only if they're not going to get in your way.'

John smiled. 'No, it means it'll get done 3 times as quickly,' he said with a wink.

Hugh turned to Ben and nodded his head in the direction of the hotel. 'You can just come back later,' he said. 'That should give you long enough to talk to Mom.' Before Ben could even answer, Hugh pointed towards the road and then turned his back on him to join Molly and John.

'Bye, Ben!' called Molly. 'Good luck!' she added before dipping the brush into the paint tin.

Ben's feet suddenly felt very sticky. 'Alright, alright,' he answered, feeling flustered. 'I'm going. You both behave for John and if there are any problems, come straight back to the hotel, together,' he demanded.

'I promise,' said Hugh, placing his hand on his heart.

For the first time, Ben wished there was an emergency to deal with, so that he didn't have to do what he needed to do. But everything remained calm and perfect. 'Darn it,' he muttered under his breath as he made his way back along the edge of the loch, towards the hotel. With every step, his heart started to beat more quickly.

As Ben approached the hotel entrance, he glanced back down the road: *That seemed to take a lot less time than on the way there*, he thought, as he momentarily paused to catch his breath. 'Come on, Ben!' he said firmly to himself. 'You can do this. It's the right time.' He tried to coax his body back into the hotel but his feet remained frozen to the spot. He closed his eyes and felt the ground beneath his life quiver and shake.

'Are you alright?' inquired a sweet voice next to him. Ben slowly opened his eyes to find Ally standing in front of him, looking concerned. 'You look very pale. You're not going to pass out on me, are you?' she asked, wanting only one answer.

Ben smiled weakly and shook his head. He reached down, laced his fingers between hers and began to guide her back down towards the edge of the loch. He slipped off his coat and wrapped it around her shoulders. Ally remained quiet as they began to walk along the water's edge. She cautiously looked across at Ben. She really didn't know what he was thinking and it unnerved her.

'There's something I need to tell you,' said Ben after what seemed like an eternity. 'But I'm so afraid to, in case it ruins everything that we have become. But to not tell you would be like watching poison ivy slowly grow around our love, and gradually suffocate it until it no longer existed.' Ben kept his gaze on the shore as his footsteps crunched along the pebbles. Ally's grip got tighter and tighter, but she remained silent and focused only on putting one foot in front of the other.

Ben let out a deep sigh and Ally saw a tear roll down his cheek. 'Do you remember asking me why I became so agitated in the town, especially where the traffic lights were?' he asked.
'Yes,' replied Ally simply.
Ben's footsteps paused a moment but he continued to walk. 'Well, there was an accident there. It was the talk of the town. Actually, it still is in some ways,' he explained. His voice began to crack as more tears fell. His attempt to push down the growing lump in his throat wasn't working.
'It's OK,' soothed Ally. 'It can't be that bad.' Ally stopping him and forced him to look into her eyes.

Ben met Ally's gaze and he crumbled with an overwhelming feeling of love for the person in front of him, and his unfathomable devotion. He felt he would have no future if she wasn't in it. 'It is bad,' corrected Ben. 'And worse.' He was now no longer able to stand and he collapsed to his knees. Ally instinctively sank down and wrapped herself protectively around him as he wept. She wished so deeply that she could take the pain away. 'It was all my fault,' sobbed Ben. 'I should never have shouted at her. Then she would never have driven off that night and none of it would have even happened.'

Ally slowly pulled away so she could hear his words. Confusion washed over her. 'Honey,' she said gently. 'You're not making any sense. Please start from the beginning. If there is one thing that I am certain about it, it is that our love can withstand all life's growing pains.'
Ben sat down on his bottom and pulled his knees up to his chest. In that moment, he looked like a lost, little boy. 'We had been together for some time,' he began. 'And things weren't going very well, but we were both young. We were having another fight. They were becoming more and more frequent, and when we fought, it was like two bulls at logger-heads together. We threw the most cutting words at each other, usually about how I was away too much,' he continued, lowering his head.

'That night, I remember slamming my hand down on the table in frustration. She picked up the dinner plates and threw them in the sink. The sound of smashing echoed around the kitchen, and then she just stormed out. I didn't go after her. I was just so angry with her. I was away so much because I was trying to build the ranch up, so that it could take care of both of us. I was doing it for us. Anyway, I listened to the car start up and then screech off down the road. The next thing I remember is picking up the broken plates from the sink and looking at the clock on the wall. Three hours had passed since she left, which was unusual for her. Normally she would have come back before then. So I finished clearing everything up but I was starting to get more and more worried. Just as I was about to grab my keys, the phone rang. I froze, of course thinking the worst. I picked up the phone and heard my dad's voice. He was telling me that I needed to get to the hospital because there had been an accident.' Ben's shoulders shook as he surrendered to the horror he felt inside.

Ally remained motionless. Ben couldn't look at her. He was terrified of seeing the look on her face that he never wanted to see, but knew he deserved. 'I don't remember that drive to the hospital,' he continued through his tears. 'It was a complete blur. But when I got there, I found Dad by the side of her bed. She was OK. She just had a few cuts and bruises, but there was this look in her eyes that made my whole body shiver and turn cold. She turned over onto her side and faced away from me. I could feel myself getting angry with her all over again, but because I was so afraid. Dad took me by the arm and out into the corridor. He sat me down on a chair. I hope to never ever again hear the words that he spoke next.' Ben stopped as the lump in his throat finally reached his mouth and blocked anymore words.

He fought the emotion though and continued. 'Dad explained that he had been at the diner when he saw her car speeding so fast down towards the lights. Apparently she drove straight through a red light. She collided with a truck and trailer that she clearly hadn't seen coming. The guy in the truck was a neighbouring rancher and he was transporting some of his horses. Dad said there was this awful noise of crumbling metal and screeching brakes. Panic ran through the whole town as people rushed out to help. The other guy had a broken leg from where her car had collided with his door. The trailer had flipped on its side. The horse's wounds were too severe and it was decided that the kindest thing would be to put them down. She had been knocked unconscious but when she awoke, she had a cut on her head, but her seat was covered in blood.'

Ally gasped as the sudden realisation of what this meant dawned on her. 'She was pregnant,' she whispered.

Ben nodded. 'I didn't know,' he said sadly. 'She hadn't told me. What we found out later was that she had also been drinking. They tested her blood on arrival at the hospital and she was three times over the limit. I should never have shouted at her. Then she would never have left the house and all of that would never have happened.' Ben placed his hands over his head and he rocked back and forth.

'Hold on,' said Ally. 'You feel this was all your fault?' she asked, completely bewildered.

'But it is. It is all my fault,' stated Ben. 'I should have stopped her. I should have taken the keys off her. Instead, I let her drive off, knowing she wasn't thinking straight.' Ben felt the guilt crunch and twist every part of his body.

'Just stop!' cried Ally. 'You absolute donut!' She lifted her hands up in the air in protest. 'Yes, you had a part to play, but she was a fully grown woman. She was fully capable of making her own decision. Yes, you argued. But did you make her drive too fast? Did you force her to drink? Did you make her run a red? They are the consequences that she has got to live with, not you.'

'But, if none of that had happened, my child would still be alive,' Ben sobbed.

Ally paused. She didn't know what to say. She watched as his guilt cloaked his love and light, until all that was left, was darkness. 'It was an accident,' she said. 'No one could have known that would happen. But I do know something. We all have arguments and we all get angry at times, and yes, on occasion, do some reckless things. But to keep carrying this guilt around, like a ball and chain, well that's stupid. It's very real but not at all necessary. Life was lost, but also lives were saved - she was OK and so was the guy in the other truck.' Ally was trying desperately to help Ben see the truth.

'We never spoke after that day,' said Ben lifelessly. 'When she got out of hospital, she came and collected her things, and was gone. But every time I drive to those traffic lights, I see the nightmare replay in my mind, and I feel the pain like it was only yesterday.' Ally remained silent. *This is delusional*, she thought. But as she looked at Ben's face, so marked with despair, she knew it was real for him: *But how can an incident like this be taken so out of context?*

'Have you spoken to you dad about it since?' Ally asked gently.

'A little, straight after it had happened, but we

always just ended up disagreeing,' whispered
Ben. 'So, that's why you are so calm all the time,'
stated Ally. 'Huh, that makes so much sense now.
Let me guess. Your dad thinks you're a donut
too? But with extra sprinkles of guilt on top, for
good measure,' she chuckled.
Ben shot her a disapproving look and Ally got the
hint. 'Not the right time for jokes then?' she said
sheepishly.
Ben shook his head.

'I'll understand if you don't want to be with me
anymore now, you know,' said Ben as a fresh tear
rolled down his cheek.
Ally stopped a moment, scooped up her thoughts
and wondered: *how on earth is this a deal
breaker*? 'Right, enough!' she finally said, sternly.
She got to her feet and held out both of her
hands for Ben to take. But he remained
motionless. This wasn't going to wash so Ally
grabbed his hands and lifted his lifeless body to
its feet. She pulled him to the edge of the loch.
'Look! Look in the loch,' she demanded. Ben's
focused remained on his feet. 'Ben, please look
for me,' she repeated, a little more softly this
time.

Ben still didn't move. 'Right then,' said Ally and
she swiftly moved behind him. Before Ben could

do anything, she gave him an almighty shove and then watched the dead weight of him plummet into the water. As he landed, a tidal wave surged out from his body, at all angles. 'A bit of tough love is what's needed here,' Ally said, pretending to dust off her hands in triumph.

As Ben's body hit the cold water, it sent a lightning bolt through his heart. He gasped for air and his body catapulted into shock. His mind was cleared of all thoughts and he experienced the same feeling he had when he stood by the hospital bed. He flapped his hands, and his feet frantically sought something to stand on. But, each time he found a footing, he slipped on the slimy rocks. Ben felt panic begin to take over and his body shook vigorously with the cold. He closed his eyes and heard a faint whisper: *stop fighting to keep me alive. Let me go.* In that moment, Ben's arms began to calm, his feet stopped seeking solid ground and he felt himself surrender.

Ally watched Ben finally become still and she shuffled anxiously. 'Come on, Ben. You can do it. Come on, let it go,' she whispered encouragingly. Ben felt a peace begin to seep into his body and he no longer felt cold. He no longer felt the guilt. He didn't feel anything at all. He let his body suspend itself in the water. In this exact moment, between his past and his future, he no longer fought for air. Ally became worried and started to walk closer to the water's edge. Ben rolled over onto his back and angled his face towards the sky. He took in a deep, long breath and filled his body up with life. The sunlight warmed and illuminated his skin. The feeling was like that of love.

He slowly opened his eyes. His body no longer felt like his. It felt lighter as it floated on top of the water. The sunshine began to warm each part of it, filling it with love and light and he realised, for the first time, that he felt free. Ally started to wade in up to her ankles, pulling Ben out of his trance. When he heard the movement of the water, he suddenly became aware of his surroundings and slowly lowered his legs. His feet found a hold on the shore bed and he stood up. Water droplets dripped off his body, like tears. They sparkled in the sunlight as they fell back into the water. Ben glided towards Ally who was standing with her arms open wide. As he reached her, she pulled him in and squeezed him tightly. 'Welcome home, my love,' she whispered in his ear.

Ben nestled his head into her neck and Ally felt his fingertips grasp her clothing. Their embrace defined how they both felt. In this moment, words were not needed. Ben slowly lifted his head and stared deeply into Ally's eyes. They were bottomless lagoons of love and he nodded in acknowledgement and agreement. They hugged and kissed in celebration of this victory.

Ally finally broke the silence. 'We best go and rescue John from all Hugh's questions,' Ally said, beaming with pride at Ben's strength. They paddled back to the shore and Ben's clothes stuck to his body. He held up his arms and surveyed the damage.

Ally placed his jacket back around his shoulders. 'I'll run you a bath when we get back,' she promised.

They took each other's hand as they walked in silence. They both wanted to savour the feelings that were erupting inside as they watched the boat-lined jetty get nearer. 'Hello! Anyone there?' shouted Ally.

'Round here, Mom,' responded Hugh immediately. Ben and Ally made their way around the back of the cabin, and as they turned the corner, they saw Hugh and Molly standing proudly next to a gleaming boat.

'Umm, Monkey? Wasn't the paint supposed to go on the boat?' Ally asked jokily as she surveyed a now multi-coloured Hugh before her.

'Oh, Mom, that's a rubbish joke,' responded Hugh. 'Do you like it though?' he said pointing his paint brush towards the boat.

Ally smiled. 'It looks brilliant!' she gushed.
Hugh then looked across at Ben who was still
dripping with water. He cocked his head to the
side and Ben smiled. 'I am not even going to ask,'
said Hugh, shaking his head.
'Ally!' called a voice from behind.
'Hello, you,' said Ally as Molly came into view.
'Ben! Why are you so wet?' Molly exclaimed as
she screeched to a halt in front of him.
'Needed a bit of a shove to get my piece of luck
back,' replied Ben with a smile, shrugging his
shoulders.
'OK,' said Molly, feeling a little baffled.
'You have got two hard workers there,'
interrupted John. 'They haven't stopped all day.'
'Well, thank you for letting them help,' Ally said
sympathetically.
'Anytime,' replied John as he walked towards the
boat.

'Hey, Ben,' said Hugh. 'Can we take Destiny out
on the water?'
'Who's Destiny?' asked Ally in confusion.
Hugh slapped his forehead leaving a smudge of
paint behind. 'Oh, Mom,' he tutted. 'It's the name
of the boat.'
'Of course it is. How silly of me,' replied Ally,

feigning ignorance.

Ben glanced across at John. 'Any chance we could take her out at sunrise?'

'Sure,' agreed John. 'I'll leave the key in the boat. Just come down whenever you want.'

Ben looked across at Hugh. 'Is that alright for you, Chief?' he asked.

Hugh and Molly bounced up and down. 'Yes! Yes! Yes!' they cried in unison.

'OK. OK, calm down,' said Ally, motioning for them to stand still. 'We had better be heading back now. Some of us need to have a shower before dinner.' She glanced across at Ben with a wink.

'OK,' replied Molly. She and Hugh put down their paint brushes and held out their hands to John. 'Thank you, John,' they said.

John shook each of their hands, covering himself in paint too. 'Anytime,' he replied kindly.

Ally wrapped her arm around Molly as they turned and headed back to the road. Hugh and Ben followed closely behind. 'So, have you had a good day?' Ally asked as Molly skipped by her side, holding and swinging her hand as she went. Molly nodded and smiled. 'How about we all get dressed up tonight, to celebrate?' Ally suggested. Molly slowed to a walk. 'What are we celebrating?' she asked curiously.

Ally paused for a moment. 'Being lucky,' she decided.

Molly bounced back into a skip. 'Yes!' she agreed. 'That sounds like a brilliant idea!' She let go of Ally's hand and ran ahead, disappearing through the entrance of the hotel, quickly followed by Hugh and Ben.

'Bagsie first in the shower,' shouted Hugh.

'Not if I get there before you,' Ben said, tickling Hugh as he tried to run past.

Ally chuckled as she thought to herself: *I wonder what my piece of luck will be*?

As Ben soaked in the bath, he watched Ally put on her makeup in the bathroom mirror. He looked at her as she lifted up onto her tiptoes and brushed on her mascara. 'You look so beautiful,' he said in admiration.

Ally glanced at him in the mirror, and smiled. 'Thank you,' she replied. She put on her lipstick and left a red kiss mark on his cheek as she went back into the bedroom.

Ally wandered into Molly and Hugh's room. Hugh was wearing his shirt and a pair of jeans. 'Well, don't you scrub up well?' she declared as she readjusted his collar. Hugh blushed and disappeared to find Ben. Molly then appeared out of the bathroom wearing her favourite blue dress and a look of thunder. 'What's the matter?' asked Ally.

Molly stomped her way across to Ally. 'I can't get it right,' she grumbled as she held up the hairclip.

Ally smiled. 'Here, let me help,' she offered as she crouched down. She gathered Molly's hair up, tied it neatly into a bun and secured it in place with the clip. 'There,' she said. 'Perfection.' Ally stood back and admired Molly. 'You are a stunning young lady, Miss Molly.'

Molly scooted across and hugged Ally. But Ally became distracted by a sweet smell that was becoming very familiar. She turned around to see Ben standing there.

They paused a moment. 'Always taking my breath away,' Ally said as she proudly took Ben's hand. 'Shall we?' said Ben as he motioned towards the door.

'Absolutely,' agreed Ally and her heels clipped across the floor. Molly and Hugh darted around Ally and Ben as they bounded down the stairs towards the restaurant.

'Hello again,' greeted their waiter from breakfast. 'Table for four please,' asked Hugh.

'No problem. This way,' he gestured politely. 'Did

you manage to find John?' he inquired.

'Yes and we went to the island and we painted one of the boats!' Molly answered rapidly.

Ben and Ally reached the table and Ben pulled Ally's chair out for her, before taking his own seat. They all hungrily perused their menus. 'Can I take your drinks order for now?' asked the waiter.

Ben looked up. 'Could we please have a bottle of champagne with two glasses, and two lemonades in champagne glasses?'

'Of course, Sir,' replied the waiter and promptly disappeared.

'Right, you two. Do you know what you would like?' Ally asked as her stomach rumbled.

Hugh scanned the menu. 'Fish and chips for me,' he answered.

'Make that two,' Molly added before placing down her menu.

Ben continued to study his menu as Hugh placed his clasped hands on the table. 'So, Mom. You're the only one left to find your luck,' he said bluntly.

Ally stopped a moment. 'Maybe I have already found my luck,' she responded knowingly.

Hugh scowled. 'Nope. You haven't,' he said with authority.

Ally was about to engage in the discussion when the waiter arrived. 'Here you go. One bottle of champagne,' he announced.

Molly and Hugh became lost in a discussion about plans for when they returned to the ranch. Ben gave the waiter their order and then poured a glass of champagne for Ally and one for himself. 'Here's to tough love,' he said raising his eyebrows.
Ally blushed. 'It worked though,' she sniggered as their glasses chimed.
Molly and Hugh lifted their glasses too. 'Here is to being the luckiest people ever,' exclaimed Hugh and they all clinked their glasses together. They had descended into an easy conversation when the waiter arrived with their dinner. They allowed their taste buds to tingle with delight.

'Are we all finished?' asked the waiter when he reappeared a short while later.
'Clean plates,' said Hugh, proudly holding his up.
'I see,' replied the waiter. 'Well done, wee man,' he congratulated as he went around collecting the rest of the plates. 'Is there anything else I can get you?' he asked.
They were all a little too full to move. But Molly slid a camera from under the table and lifted it up towards the waiter. 'Please could you take a photo for me to add to my memory book?' she asked.

'Of course,' said the waiter. He placed the empty plates down on a nearby table and took hold of the camera. 'All huddle together,' he instructed. Hugh and Molly leant further in. 'Cheese!' they all said as they heard the click of the button.

'There you go, little lady,' said the waiter as he handed the camera back to Molly.
'Thank you,' she replied. She took the camera and placed it back on her lap.
'Well, I think we should all have an early night if we are to get up at sunrise,' Ben suggested.
Hugh groaned. 'I am so full. I don't think I can make it up the stairs,' he said, clutching his stomach.
'Don't worry, Hugh,' reassured Molly with a giggle. 'We can just roll you.' They all finally got up from the table, waved goodbye to the waiter and made their way upstairs to bed.

'Wakey-wakey.' Molly felt a warm hand on her shoulder gently rocking her. 'It's time to get up.'
Molly rolled over. 'It's still dark outside,' she mumbled sleepily.
'It's time to ride our destiny,' continued the voice. Molly's eyes shot open as she remembered. She swung herself around and sat on the edge of the mattress. She found Ally crouched down by the side her bed. Molly scanned the rest of the room.

'Where's Hugh?' she asked with concern.
'Next door, with Ben,' Ally whispered softly.
Molly focused a little more and saw that Ally was dressed. She pulled her clothes from the end of the bed. 'Why didn't you wake me sooner?' she asked. 'You are all dressed and ready,' she added, frustrated to be last.

'There's no rush,' reassured Ally as she passed Molly a jumper. 'I still haven't had my first cup of tea,' she added, lightening the mood.
Molly calmed. 'Oh, OK,' she said, slowing down. Ally made her way back into the other room and was handed a fresh cup of tea by Hugh. 'Thank you, Monkey,' Ally said, gratefully cupping it in her hands and letting the warmth radiate up her arms. Hugh put on his coat and hat, and Ben handed Ally hers. She reluctantly put her cup of tea down and pulled them on.

'OK, everyone! I'm ready!' declared Molly as she marched into the room.
'So are we,' said Hugh and he began to herd Ben and Ally towards the door. 'Come on! Let's go, otherwise we will miss it,' he ordered impatiently. They all walked quietly down to reception and were greeted by a lady. She was sitting behind the desk and her face was illuminated by the desk lamp. 'We'll be back soon,' Hugh

announced as he continued to push everyone out the entrance. Hugh and Molly burst into life as they began to run towards John's boats. Ben and Ally lengthened their strides, but by the time they had reached the jetty, Hugh and Molly had already put on their life jackets and were in position. John had kindly left the jackets in the boat for them. Ben held out his hand for Ally as she stepped into the boat. She had barely sat down before a life jacket was thrust at her. 'You have to wear one of these,' Hugh insisted.

'OK, OK, give me chance,' said Ally as she took it from him. Ben then climbed in, scooped up his life jacket and headed towards the back of the boat. Ally shuffled to find a more comfortable position. 'Everyone ready?' Ben shouted from the back of the boat.
'Aye-aye, Captain,' Molly called in response. The boat's engine came to life and Ben navigated it away from the jetty. He used the natural light from the stars and the moon which were lighting up the water, just enough to see.

The boat cut effortlessly through the water and Ben began to ease off the throttle, before turning the engine off completely. They listened to the clinking of the chain as he slowly lowered the anchor into the water. They all gazed up at thousands of sparkles of starlight in the black sky and sat in silence to better hear the night's chorus. The boat bobbed gently up and down in the water. They watched and waited. All there was to do, in that moment in time, was just be.

The cloak of darkness slowly lightened as the sun began to rise behind the boat. The sky displayed an array of colours: reds, purples, oranges and yellows. The glorious sphere of light rose above the crest of the horizon and the stars slowly disappeared. The night's chorus played its final notes and the birds started to sing, to herald the beginning of a new day. They all watched, completely mesmerised, as the colours in the sky transformed and got brighter. Ally looked down at the reflections in the water. She could see the shimmering silhouettes of Hugh, Molly and Ben, surrounded by the radiance of the sunrise. She smiled to herself as Mother Nature showed her the brilliance that was before her and framed this moment. It was a memory that would forever hang on the wall of her heart.

Ally took a slow, steady breath in. She saw, for the first time, that what she had wished for had already come true. They were creating this memory together, as a family. A piece slotted back into her heart and, once more, her luck was restored.

7 FOOTPRINTS OF FAITH

Ally snapped out of her daze and realised that everyone was staring at her. She coughed nervously and they all smiled. 'We were waiting to see when you would get your piece of luck back,' Molly said, tapping her feet excitedly.
'Well, I know it has returned,' Ally replied with a joyous smile.

The sun climbed higher in the sky and fully lit the land. 'Shall we head back for some breakfast?' asked Ben, tapping his stomach.
They all nodded in unison. 'I am so hungry,' cried Hugh dramatically, pretending to faint with starvation. Ben pulled up the anchor and lay it in the bottom of the boat. He started up the engine and the boat soared towards the jetty. Ally grabbed clumps of her hair and tried to hold it

back as it tossed and turned in the wind.

As they approached the jetty, they saw a figure making its way down towards them. Hugh and Molly began to wave frantically. 'Morning, John!' they shouted at the top of their lungs. John lifted off his tweed cap and waved it in the air in greeting.

Before even being asked, Hugh took hold of the rope and got ready to throw it to John. Ben slowed Destiny down and slotted her back in line. John took hold of the rope and secured it to the jetty. He held out his hand and, one by one, guided everybody off the boat. 'Cracking morning to watch the sunrise,' John said with a smile. 'It was spectacular!' Hugh agreed, raising his hands up in the air.

The sound of their footsteps on the wooden jetty echoed around the loch. When they reached the cabin, Molly collected the life jackets, ran inside and hung them up. 'We best be heading back to the hotel for some breakfast,' said Ally. 'We've got a long drive ahead of us after that.' She pulled Hugh in for a hug.

'And, you did it again, Hugh. That was another incredible map of dreams,' Ben said as he ruffled his hair.

Hugh smiled shyly. 'You're welcome,' he muttered.

Molly bounced up behind Hugh and leapt onto him – a true Molly-hug. 'Thank you, brother. You're the best!' she exclaimed as she squeezed the air out of him.

'Bye, John,' said Ben. 'Thanks for everything.' He shook John's hand warmly.

'Anytime you're back up this way, don't forget to drop in and say hi,' replied John kindly.

'Absolutely,' agreed Ben with an enthusiast nod.

They made their way along the road, walking a little slower this time to savour every moment, and store the images in their minds. 'You know, I think I am starting to understand it,' said Molly as she swung her arms.

'What's that?' Ally asked.

'The lessons life gives us to help build up our strength,' Molly explained. 'It's pretty clever really. Because life won't give us something we can't handle. We might think we won't make it through, because it's a lot of effort. But actually, if you keep chipping away at it, you become stronger, and you do make it through. And you become a better person too. All be it a little tired at the end though,' she concluded.

'There she goes again. Wise Molly, teaching us all life's truths,' Ally said, as she pretended to tickle her. She gave her a proud kiss on the top of her head.

They stepped through the entrance of the hotel, now alight with the morning sun. 'Good morning,' greeted a familiar voice from the doorway of the restaurant. 'Would you like your usual table?' Hugh beamed a giant smile. 'You are my hero,' he said to the waiter. 'Lead the way.'

They made their way to the table and sat down in their seats. 'Same as usual?' asked the waiter. He didn't think he would need his note pad and pen this time. Ally nodded her agreement and Ben tucked a piece of stray hair behind her ear. 'So, is everything all sorted for heading back tomorrow?' he asked gently.
'I think so,' replied Ally. 'All the paperwork is complete, money transferred, belongings packed. We are ready to head home.' The word *home* now felt so wonderful, like a sanctuary, a piece of heaven.

'I'm looking forwards to going home and seeing Tom and Grandpa Billy,' Molly said. A wave of pure relief washed over her. The fear of not being able to stay with Ally had been well and truly vanquished.
'What shall we do when we get back?' Hugh

asked as he began to plan.

'I think take a break and just enjoy life,' Ally said, exhausted.

'Yeah, it'll be nice that the only things we have to accomplish are eating, sleeping and pooing,' shouted Hugh mischievously.

Ally frowned her disproval.

'What?' Hugh protested. 'It's true. You would become very poorly if you didn't.'

The waiter returned with their breakfasts. As he placed them on the table he turned to Ben. 'And here is some extra toast for you,' he said with a smile.

'Thank you,' breathed Ben, admiring the feast in front of him.

'Shall I reserve a table for dinner?' the waiter asked, glancing back at the diary.

'I am afraid not,' replied Ally. 'We will be heading off after this. Thank you for everything though. You have treated us like royalty,' she added gratefully.

'Well, that was what I was instructed to do by a lady called Jane,' the waiter said as he recalled the phone call. 'She told me what you had been through and I think her words were: *you best treat them like royalty otherwise I will be up there myself to give you a talking too*,' the waiter said, pulling a mock-scared face. 'Quite a feisty woman, if I may say so.' They all erupted into laughter.

Ally put the last bite of breakfast into her mouth and chewed it slowly. She sighed with satisfaction. 'Now I am set to hit the road again,' she stated, placing her napkin down next to her empty plate.

'I'll miss this place,' said Hugh. 'It's like a hidden treasure that's there for everyone to see, but that most pass by.' He glanced out of the window and watched a bird glide along the top of the water.

'Right then, gang,' instructed Ben as he stood. 'Let's go and pack up, load up and make some tracks in that tarmac.'

'Mom, can I borrow a pen?' asked Hugh.
Ally lifted up her bag and sifted through it. 'There you go, Monkey,' she said as she handed him the located pen. Hugh delicately wrote a note on his napkin, then stood to join everyone else. He left the napkin strategically at the head of the table, for the waiter to find.

They paraded back up to their rooms and proceeded to pack their bags once more. It got a little easier each time as their load appeared lighter. Molly and Hugh took it in turns to help each other carry their bags down to the reception

where Ben and Ally were already waiting. 'Thanks, Champ,' Ben said, taking the bags out to the car. Ally was busy at the reception desk. She handed back the keys and paid their bill. 'We hope to see you again soon,' said the receptionist with a well-practised smile.
'We won't be forgetting this place in a hurry,' replied Ally as she took one final look around.

Ally made her way outside to Hugh, Molly and Ben, who were already waiting in the car. She paused on the steps of the hotel and took in one final deep breath of air. 'Is everyone settled in?' she inquired when she climbed in. 'And ready for another epic drive? Maybe this time you'll all see a bit more of it, not the back of your eyelids.' She chuckled, as she started the car and navigated it back down the country roads.

Ben watched the country rolling on by as they slipped onto the motorway and back towards the faster pace of society. He pondered to himself: *sometimes going down a new road for the first time is easier as the excitement and eagerness consume you. But, if you're going down a familiar road and you still have that same feeling, it shows that the road is the right path to take. And to keep feeling those moments of excitement on a road well-travelled, well, that's when you are truly living life to the fullest.* Ben smiled to himself at the thought.

'What are you smiling at?' Ally asked glancing across at Ben.

He reached out, placed his hand on her shoulder and gave it a squeeze. 'Just living life to the fullest,' he whispered.

'I spy with my little eye, something beginning with J,' Hugh said with a mischievous smile.

'Umm, is it jumper?' asked Molly.

'Nope,' replied Hugh a little smugly.

'Is it John?' said Molly scratching her head.

Hugh began to laugh. 'No, silly. He is back up by the loch. You'll never guess it,' he stated, beginning to feel victorious.

'Is it jewellery then?' tried Molly. Her eyes were bright with delight. Surely this was right.

Hugh shook his head. 'Nope.'

'Ben, please help me,' implored Molly.

'OK, Hugh,' Ben asserted. 'We need some clues. Can we see it now?' he asked.

'Not right now,' Hugh replied.

'Will we see it soon?' Ben continued.

'Yes, really soon,' Hugh said, getting excited.

'I've got it, I've got it!' cried Molly. 'It's Ja...' Just as Ally pulled up outside the house, Jane stepped out, holding a fresh cup of coffee. Molly vigorously pointed at her. 'It's Jane,' she said with a satisfied grin as Ally turned off the engine.

They all piled out of the car and filed into the house. 'So, how was your adventure?' asked Jane, stepping out of the way as Hugh and Molly darted through. They stood in front of her like two leaping frogs.

'It was incredible!' Molly began.

'Absolutely amazing!' continued Hugh. 'We made a wish at the waterfall and then went up to the lochs of luck where we met John and rode in Destiny.'

Ally walked into the house and hugged Jane.

'Thank you so much for lending us your car,' she said.

'The kettle's not long boiled,' Jane said and she motioned for Ally to join her in the kitchen.

Ally turned to face the leaping frogs. 'Seeing as you two have still got plenty of energy, please could you bring the bags in and put them in the living room?' she asked. 'But, only take out what you need for tonight and leave the rest down here. We have an early start in the morning to catch our flight.' Ally couldn't prevent a yawn escape from her mouth.

'Ally, I heard that from in here,' called Jane.

'Come and get a cup of tea before you fall asleep standing up,' she instructed.

Ally shuffled into the kitchen as Ben entered the

house with the first handful of bags. Molly and Hugh slipped past to gather the remaining ones and bring them inside too. 'Hi, Jane,' greeted Ben as he placed the bags down and walked into the kitchen.

Jane handed him a cup of coffee. 'Did it all go well?' she asked, eager for gossip.

'Better than any of us could have imagined,' replied Ben. 'But I'll let Hugh and Molly do the talking and show you the pictures. I know they can't wait to.'

Ally yawned again and her mouth stayed open for longer than felt comfortable. 'I am going to have to give in,' she muttered. 'Thanks again, Jane,' she said, giving her another hug.

'Always here to help,' said Jane with a smile. 'I'll see you in the morning for drop off.' Jane couldn't hide the sadness. Things felt empty without Ally and her weekly gossips over the kitchen table. Ally nodded. Another yawn thundered out and she turned and made her way upstairs.

Jane and Ben made their way through to the living room where Hugh and Molly were already flicking through the pictures. 'Do you have a printer here, Hugh?' asked Molly as she paused at the picture of them all sitting around the dinner table.

'Yeah, just in here,' confirmed Hugh and he went

to turn it on.

Molly rummaged through her bag for her memory book whilst Hugh printed off the picture. 'Here you go,' said Ben, handing Molly a pen.

Molly sat down and placed the picture on the next page. She smiled knowingly as her pen streamed across the page: *Love is there, not only just to share the good times, but to give you strength through the tough times. It is knowing that if you hold out your hand, there will always be a hand there that takes hold of it.*

She slowly closed the book and put it back into her bag. 'I am ready to go back home,' she said, hugging Ben.

Ben smiled. 'Me too,' he sighed. 'Who knows what your grandpa and Tom have been up to? Or what the ranch looks like for that matter.' Ben began to wonder. He hadn't had a single phone call since he left. It began to dawn on him, for the first time, that he didn't know how the ranch was. His anxiety bubbled away inside.

'Night-night, Jane,' said Molly as she gave Jane a hug.

'See you in a few hours,' Jane replied with a smile.

Hugh's gaze drifted casually around. Memory upon memory replayed themselves in his mind.

There were so many that were attached to this house. He, too, began to unthread each stitch that held him to this life that was no longer his.

I'll be heading off as well,' said Jane. 'Glad you got back alright,' she added as she got up and placed her cup on the coffee table.
'Thanks for getting everything ready for our return,' Ben said appreciatively.
'No problem at all,' Jane called behind her as she stepped out of the front door and into the cooling night.

Ben turned to Hugh. 'Right, Champion. I think it would be right for us to...umm...what is it you guys say? Head up the apples and pears!' Ben was clearly delighted with himself.
Hugh shook his head. 'You're a quick learner,' he acknowledged. Hugh stood up and started to make his way up the stairs. Ben locked the front door and turned off the lights. Hugh paused at the top and waited for Ben to catch up. When Ben reached the last step, Hugh flung his arms around him, and he felt Ben melt into his hug.

'See you in a few hours, Champion,' Ben said, kissing the top of Hugh's head.
Hugh meandered into his room and flicked on the light switch. The room became illuminated, and

so did his map of dreams. He, very carefully, looked at each individual picture and felt a buzz begin to build inside. *I'm not sure when I'll be back again*, he thought to himself. He put on his pyjamas, peeled back his duvet but then paused.

He stepped away from his bed, and went to find another old, empty school book, a pen and some glue. He sat down on his bed and wrote: **A Diary of my Dreams Achieved**, in big, bold letters on the front. He opened up the book to the first blank page and looked up at his wall of dreams. His gaze fell on the first photo of a plane. He carefully took it down, stuck it into his book and wrote the date next to it. He then reached up and took the photo of the country fair and rodeo, and stuck that next to it. One by one, the photos began to transfer from the wall into the book. Hugh felt a huge sense of joy. He hadn't realised just how much had been achieved since he had first created his map of dreams.

Hugh took down the final few photos of the dreams he had achieved. He flicked through his book and realised that every photo was a building block of his new life. Moment by moment, memory by memory, they all joined together to create the picture of his new life. Hugh chuckled to himself as he felt bubbles of happiness in his stomach, fizzle and pop with joy. He looked up at the photos still left on the wall. They were of the dreams he was yet to receive. He scratched his chin: *What to do with these? Do I give up on them and throw them away, or shall they come with me and be added to my other dream wall at the ranch?* He pondered this thought for a moment: *I can't give up on my dreams, because that would mean that I was giving up on myself, and those parts of me that I want to grow, or even discover.*

Hugh stood up on his bed and took down the pictures. He tucked them just behind the front cover of the book: *I'll add them to my other dream wall, when the time is right. As my past becomes a blank slate, my future is brightly decorated with opportunities, experiences, and endless possibilities.* He placed the book by his clothes, ready for packing in the morning. He finally slithered under his duvet. He pulled it up so high that only his face was showing. He blinked twice, but by the third time, his eyelids stayed shut.

Hugh lazily rolled over but his eyes shot open with surprise when he felt something by the side of him. 'Molly!' he yelled out in shock.
'Morning, Sleepy,' whispered Molly. 'It's time to go home.' She was laid by his side, already fully dressed in her coat and shoes.
Hugh scowled. 'It can't be time yet?' he muttered,

trying to soothe himself back to sleep.

Molly huffed. She was too excited to sleep anymore. 'Not quite,' she said with a cheeky grin. 'But, in 2 minutes and 17 seconds, Ally's alarm will be going off!'

Hugh pulled his duvet up around himself, trying to savour the last 2 minutes of sleep. 'Why are you so tired anyway?' asked Molly as she fidgeted beside him.

'I haven't been asleep for long,' explained Hugh. 'There was something I needed to do before we left.'

Molly looked up at the blank wall and it dawned on her what Hugh meant. She rolled over and gave him a hug. 'I am proud of you,' she whispered as she swung her legs over him. As her feet touched the ground, the sound of Ally's alarm rang out. 'Perfect timing,' Molly said, quite pleased with herself.

Molly's feet thumped to the beat of the alarm as she made her way down stairs. When she reached the bottom, she filled her lungs as full of air as she could. 'Wakey-wakey, Sleepy-heads!' she yelled at the top of her voice before disappearing into the kitchen to put the kettle on for Ally and Ben.

'I think someone is excited to be heading back to

the ranch,' said Ben with a sleepy smile as he wrapped his arms around Ally. He glanced across and was surprised to see Ally just laying there, staring up at the ceiling. He propped himself up on his elbow. 'Are you OK?' he asked gently, beginning to get concerned. Ally let out a deep, contemplative sigh. Ben's nerves grew as the moment of silence did too.

Ally blinked and her thought-trance was momentarily broken. She looked across at Ben and smiled. 'I don't know how she's done it,' Ally begun. 'I look around this place and I know that I need to the same, but I don't know if I can.' Ben stayed silent. Ally saw the worry wash across his face. 'Oh no, not like that,' she reassured. 'I can't wait to get back to the ranch and continue our life together. I just don't want to have to deal with this. I kind of wish someone would sort it all out for me so I didn't have to take the journey.' She rested her head on his chest.

'Ally, there is no point avoiding the past. It will just follow you around for the rest of your life,' stated Ben. 'Yes, it's easier to get something new and put it on top of whatever it is you want to hide. But it's so much better if you get rid of the things that you no longer want, and create space for something new.' Ben pulled her in close. 'But, you won't be going through it alone,' he soothed. 'I

will always be here, by your side, unconditionally and eternally loving you.'
He kissed her and Ally began to feel relief. 'It always seems so doable when you say it,' she said.

There was a sudden smash from downstairs. Ally and Ben looked at each other. 'I guess we aren't getting up quick enough for a certain little girl,' said Ben.
'It's OK!' called a voice from the kitchen.
A very sleepy Hugh sauntered into the bedroom. Ally sat herself up. 'Would someone go and stop the tornado,' pleaded Hugh. 'I beg you!' He fell dramatically onto the bed as Molly entered the room. She was balancing a cup in each hand, watching the fluid slosh precariously around the edges.

Ben climbed out of bed and made his way around to Molly. He took the cups from her. 'Thank you,' he said. Molly promptly turned on her heels, and ran back downstairs into the living room, to pack the last of her things. Ben handed Ally the other cup as Hugh tried to sneak into Ally and Ben's bed. 'Oh no you don't!' warned Ally. 'Go and get dressed. You can sleep on the flight. And Jane will be here soon.' Hugh hung his head low and wandered off to do what he was told.

'It's going to be a long day,' sighed Ally, sipping her tea. 'But I will give her her dues. She does make a very good cup of tea.' Ally reluctantly set down her cup, climbed out of bed and got dressed.

Ben, Ally and Hugh finally made their way downstairs to pack the last of their things. 'Hugh, is there anything you would like boxing up and posting back to the ranch?' Ally asked as they walked into the kitchen. Hugh yawned in response. 'I'll take that as a no then,' she said, ruffling his hair.

They found Molly sitting on her bag, by the front door, playing with her locket. 'Well, we're not going to forget you,' said Ben as he knelt down in front of her. Her intentions were written so clearly across her face.

Molly gave a weak smile and hugged Ben tightly. 'Knock-knock,' said Jane as she came through the front door. 'Oh, I guess you're all ready to go then?' she asked, peering down at Molly. 'Yes, we are,' replied Molly. She unravelled herself from Ben, picked up her bag and marched out to the car. Ben reached across, stuffed his toothbrush inside his bag and followed Molly.

Hugh was next to arrive. He softly waved a *hello* to Jane before grabbing his bag and getting in the car. 'What a lively bunch,' said Jane sarcastically. Ally then came into the hallway. She was frantically scanning the house and seemed nervous. 'Hey! Earth to Ally,' called Jane, waving her hand in front of her eyes. Jane grabbed hold of Ally's shoulder. 'It's going to be alright,' she soothed. 'I'll keep an eye on the place, just like before, and let you know of any emergencies.' Ally was in shock. It was so much harder to leave this time, perhaps because she no longer wanted to flee. 'OK, you're right,' said Ally. 'It's all going to be fine.' She didn't believe a single one of her own words. Jane picked up Ally's bag and made her way outside. Ally slowly followed and put her hand anxiously on the handle. The house became a time capsule of her past, yet again, patiently waiting for her return. Ally closed the door with a bang and turned the key. 'I'll save that gremlin for another day,' she whispered to herself as the lock clicked and the house became silent.

Ally climbed into the front seat, closed the door and put on her seat belt. 'Right! Ready,' she said, clapping her hands determinedly together. Jane glanced across and shook her head. 'You're a rubbish liar, Ally,' Jane said with a smile. 'Oh, come on. Drive, lady,' Ally instructed, signalling for Jane to move forwards. Jane politely obliged, sensing that it wasn't the time for anymore jokes.

The car was silent except for the sound of Hugh snoring in the back. He had fallen asleep on Ben's shoulder. Molly watched the road get busier and busier as they neared the airport. She felt the relief wash over her. She was ready to leave what once was, and delve into her new life that awaited her. 'Hey, Buddy.' Ben gently shook Hugh. 'We're here.' Hugh sleepily lifted his head as Jane slowed the car and steered it into the drop off lane.

Jane tapped Ally on the knee. 'Here we are again,' she whispered.
Molly climbed out. 'Come on, everyone. If we're quick enough, we may be able to have a hot chocolate before we get on the plane.' She made her way to the boot of the car and Hugh sluggishly slid out and joined her.
'It was great to finally meet you, Jane,' said Ben warmly. 'And I guess the next time I'll see you will be at the wedding,' he added as he gave her a hug.
'Can't wait,' replied Jane excitedly. 'I'll be the first one on the next flight as soon as you tell us the date. It will be a day to remember,' she stated with eager anticipation.

Ally made her way round the front of the car and

wrapped Jane in a huge hug. 'Thank you for always being there for me,' she sobbed. 'I couldn't have done any of this without you.'
Ally began to cry harder. 'Oh come on, you,' urged Jane. 'I think you are doing pretty well without me,' she added as she gestured towards Ben. 'Everything is going to be alright now.'
Ally looked up and wiped away her tears. 'You know what, I think you're right, Jane. You're welcome to come over anytime,' she offered. 'The door will always be open and the kettle always on.' Ally took the bag that Ben was handing to her.
Jane nodded. 'I'll see you on the big day,' she said with a wink. 'By the way, when is that?' she asked provocatively.
'No, don't you start as well,' warned Ally. 'I need a rest. One dream at a time,' she said, playfully wiggling her finger at Jane. 'Let me just get settled into this new family life first.' Ally shook her head and followed Hugh and Molly into the airport.
'See you very soon, Jane,' Ben mouthed with a thumbs up. Jane giggled with excitement as she got back into her car and drove off.

They joined the queue just as check-out opened. 'Good morning, Mam. May I please have your passports?' said a friendly lady from behind the desk. Ally slid the passports across and Ben lifted the bags onto the conveyor belt. 'Did you pack your own bags today, Mam?' asked the lady. Ally nodded as Hugh and Molly began to make their way towards security. 'Lovely. Well here are your tickets. Have a great flight,' she said as she handed back the passports with the plane tickets tucked inside.

Ben took hold of Ally's hand as they followed Hugh and Molly. 'You know, the last time I checked in there, you were just a thought, a dream, a wish. And now you're here, holding my hand as we head home,' Ally said in amazement. 'Life is magical, but only if we keep believing,' replied Ben affectionately.

They made their way through security. Molly held her breath, hoping that the scanner wouldn't beep. 'Who's up for some hot chocolate?' asked Ben.

'Yes, I am!' answered Molly before Ben had barely had chance to finish the question. 'With cream and marsh mallows on!' Molly rubbed her stomach in anticipation. Hugh was now feeling more awake and he began to peer into the different shops as they walked by. He took in the array of goodies and sparkly objects, but it was his boots by the front door of the ranch that he longed for the most.

'I'll go and fetch the hot chocolates while you guys take a seat,' offered Ben and he disappeared into a throng of people, all with the same thing in mind, apparently. Hugh, Molly and Ally found some seats and they watched the planes take off.

'I wonder where they are all going,' Hugh pondered curiously.

Ally glanced across. 'Anywhere and everywhere,' she said. 'Every destination on the planet is only a flight away.' She winked at Hugh, and his adventurous side.

'Here you go, everyone,' said Ben as he arrived back with a tray of hot drinks. 'I went for the ones with extra topping, seeing as we are celebrating,' he said as he sat down next to Ally.

They raised up their hot chocolates. 'Here's to the dream-team,' said Hugh proudly. 'For overcoming all, but most of all, for doing it together.'

They all sipped their drinks as more and more people filtered through into the waiting area. Ally kept a keen eye on the check-in desk. The air stewardess had started to get people into position, ready to load up the plane. 'You best drink up,' she said, gulping down the last of her hot chocolate. 'I think they are going to announce that we can board soon.' Ben looked in the same direction as Ally.

Molly and Hugh tipped up their cups and stuck out their tongues, to get the last drops of melted cream. 'Finished,' they said in unison.
'Gate 17 is now open for boarding,' said an efficient voice over the tannoy. 'Could first class passengers please make their way to the desk first and then all other passengers will be announced by seat numbers.'
'Come on, you guys,' said Ben as he stood up. 'We best get going.'
Ally looked up at him. 'There's no rush,' she replied. 'We won't be boarding just yet.'
Ben smirked. 'Come on, Hugh and Molly. Let's board the plane.'
'Ben, wait,' said Ally with a little more urgency this time. 'Boarding is for first class passengers only.'
Ben pulled out her passport and held her ticket in front of her eyes. 'Yes, that's correct. And that means you.'
Ally's mouth dropped open in shock as Ben ushered her towards the desk. He handed over the passports and tickets while Ally looked from him to the ticket and back to him again.

'But how? When?' she finally managed to stammer. Ben took hold of her hand as they walked down the tunnel, not saying a word.
'Good morning,' said a very smiley stewardess. 'If

you would like to follow me.' She glanced at their tickets and guided them down the aisle. Ally melted into her seat. She felt like a queen.

'I wonder what will be waiting for us back at the ranch,' Hugh pondered as they followed the stewardess.

Molly slotted into her seat by the window and looked at Hugh, straight in the eye. 'I don't know what is around the next corner,' she said. 'But I know now, that no matter what it is, I have got...' she paused a moment.

'The strength to succeed.'

Can You Help?

We would love to hear what you thought about the book.

1. Go to Amazon;

2. Type 'Naomi Sharp' into the search box and press enter;

3. Click on the book;

4. Scroll down until you reach the star chart;

5. Click the button and write a review.

Every review received is a wonderful gift each day. Thank you.

With gratitude,

Naomi

8 ABOUT THE AUTHOR

www.naomisharpauthor.com

Naomi began making notes when she was just 10 years old. Still today, she always has a notebook to hand, ready to jot down the next profound thought or idea.

It wasn't until 6 years later that Naomi would write her first book: Living Life With The Glass Half Full. In it, she shares her story of changing life's adversity into lessons learned. No sooner had she finished that book, she was inspired to write her next: A Diary Of Dreams, her first work of fiction. Naomi describes the experience as, 'downloading a story, like a movie was playing in front of me and I was writing down what was happening, moment by moment.'

Naomi's passion to inspire people to heal and find hope and happiness continues to grow. So, she continues to write. She feels that storytelling is an incredible way to pass on wisdom and life's truths.

Naomi trained as an Occupational Therapist but became fascinated by horses. In particular, their ability to help people heal, not only physically, but also mentally and emotionally. Her passion for understanding how we can help our bodies to heal and our dreams to become reality has brought some breath taking experiences into her life. She has had the opportunity to meet some incredible people and visit some memorable places.

During the day, Naomi also runs her therapy centre for individuals with a mental, physical or emotional disability. These people can come and spend time with horses, and celebrate what makes them unique.

9 OTHER BOOKS BY NAOMI SHARP

A Diary Of Dreams (Universal Series Book 1)

A journey to remembering that dreams can come true.

Finding love and happiness, following the death of a family member, by living your dreams. Hugh watched his mom's happiness dissolve away as a dark depression took hold. All Ally could see was the new absence in her life, a love that was no longer there. Hugh dreamed of his mom finding her happiness, falling in love and rediscovering the magic of life. He visualised her allowing the lost love to transform as they embarked on a new chapter in life. Hugh decided to create a map of dreams, a vision board, of all the things he wanted to happen in his life. This resulted in an adventure that took him and Ally to meet the people they needed to meet and visit the places they needed to go. It took them towards dreams they wanted to experience, and they discovered how truly magical life could be. This book will help to inspire you to plan for and dream of the life you truly desire. It will empower women and children to have the courage to follow their heart's desires, thus enabling their ambitions in life to flourish. An incredible story of how family, dreams and love can help you achieve anything you want.

A Locket of Love (Universal Series Book 2)

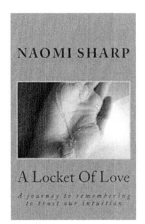

A journey to remembering to follow our intuition.

As Nana O waited for Molly to arrive, she sat in her usual chair by the fire. She twiddled her thumbs and began to think about the story that she was going to tell, about a locket and the secret it holds.

Molly arrived, feeling awkward and shuffling her feet. She didn't want to be there, but sat down on the stool in front of Nana O anyway. She quickly became captivated as the story began to unfold. Nana O told Molly about a single locket that held a secret. That secret would help Molly to remember and understand how to follow her own intuition. Molly begins to follow it, day by day, and her life begins to transform. She slowly becomes the person she was meant to be. She is closely followed, on her journey, by her two best friends, Layla and Dillon, who are always there, supporting her along the way.

Throughout the book there are golden nuggets of wisdom which will help you to remember life truths that may have been forgotten. This is the second book in the universal series, looking at the law of oneness.

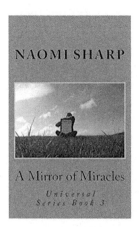

A Mirror of Miracles (Universal Series Book 3)

A journey to remembering the power of self-image.

Hugh paces the living room, waiting for the arrival of Molly. Butterflies swirl around in his stomach. As the truck pulls up in front of the house, Hugh leaps into action and sprints to the front door. Molly steps out of the truck and Hugh heads straight for her. Molly flings her arms around him as Hugh whispers, 'Welcome home.'

As Molly and Hugh stand in front of the mirror, Billy begins to reveal the next of life's truths. This starts a life changing adventure as they begin to understand and practise the new truth.

Molly's parents announce they are heading back to England early, leaving Molly with Ally, Ben and Hugh. None of them realise what is waiting for them all just around the next corner, causing life to never be the same again.

Living Life With The Glass Half Full

An inspiring true story of how a young girl chooses to learn from life's adversity with the help of horses. She travels to Ireland, France and America to understand how to live a better, happier life, and to understand what it truly means to heal. The story follows her from her younger days, causing mischief in nursery, through to the frustration of being dyslexic in school. This leads to her whole world being turned around with a profound realisation. All the while, different horses are guiding her path with their constant friendship and companionship. They continually highlight some of the facts of life that Naomi has picked up along the way. The book includes a bonus feature for your own personal development. It provides ways for you to analyse your life's problems and turn them into positives, with surprising ease. It encourages you to work through your own challenges by changing your perceptions on how you view life and adversity. This book provides a true account of how the adventure of life is more about using your lessons to help dreams become reality, rather than allowing adversity to become your future.

40 Days Transforming Your Life

Are you ready for the journey of a lifetime? Have you received enough of life's adversity? Do you feel your back is up against the wall?

Help has arrived!

In this 'how-to' book, you will discover a *40 day process* that will help you and your life to transform. You will be taken from a place of despair to a place where dreams come true.

You won't be doing this journey alone though. Every day, there is a short chapter which will look at what the day ahead has in store, as you move up and down the emotional scale. In this 'how-to' book, you will explore what it means to change from the inside out. It will provide pearls of wisdom, to keep you inspired and motivated to move forwards.

Aspects included in 40 Days Transforming Your Life:

~ Letting go of past experiences;
~ Loving yourself and your strengths;
~ Learning to set a goal or dream;
~ Setting up your routine for success;
~ Celebrating your achievements;
~ Worry no longer being part of your day.

40 Days Transforming Your Life, by Naomi Sharp, will help you develop a simple but sustainable routine to reaching your goals, transforming your life, and living your dreams.

Printed in Great Britain
by Amazon